Other Books

Scanguards '
Samson's Lovely Mortal
Amaury's Hellion
Gabriel's Mate
Yvette's Haven
Zane's Redemption
Quinn's Undying Rose
Oliver's Hunger
Thomas's Choice
Silent Bite (novella)
Cain's Identity
Luther's Return

Out of Olympus Series
A Touch of Greek
A Scent of Greek
A Taste of Greek

Eternal Bachelors Club
Lawful Escort
Lawful Lover
Lawful Wife
One Foolish Night
One Long Embrace

Lover Uncloaked (Stealth Guardians, Book 1)

Venice Vampyr (Novellas 1 – 4)

Just the Sex, Ma'am

A collection of steamy scenes from
Tina Folsom's novels

NEW YORK TIMES BESTSELLING AUTHOR
TINA FOLSOM

Cover design © 2015 by Tina Folsom

Just the Sex, Ma'am
© 2010 – 2015 by Tina Folsom

Amaury's Hellion

Scanguards Vampires

NEW YORK TIMES BESTSELLING AUTHOR

TINA FOLSOM

"Good night, Nina."

He turned and stalked toward the door, anxious to leave quickly so he wouldn't lose his resolve.

"You can't leave now!" There was a twinge of desperation in her voice. Had he also sounded like that the night before?

"Watch me." Amaury stepped through the door and shut it behind him. He heard Nina's voice calling after him as he walked through the dark corridor, but he didn't turn back.

When he walked into the cool night air, he braced himself for a moment. God, he wanted that woman. He'd tasted her arousal and her blood, and both were the sweetest tastes he'd ever had. He could lose himself in her.

At first it had seemed like a good plan to do to her what she'd done to him: arouse her and then leave her unsatisfied. But touching her this intimately, tasting her arousal, and feeling her response to him, had gotten him more randy than a sailor after a twelve-month tour at sea. And half as refined. The way he felt right now, he'd do her in the street in full view of the entire city and not give a rat's ass about exposure. Or common decency.

He had to get out of here before he gave into his urges, went back, threw her onto the floor and took her like the savage he was, not caring if she wanted him or not. Only eager to still his own lust.

Amaury clicked the remote for the car and heard the familiar beeps. His black Porsche was parked only a few yards away. Normally, he didn't use the car for short trips downtown, but Gabriel and the others were expecting him for the first set of one-on-one interviews with the employees they had selected during the staff meetings.

The car door was jerked out of his hand and slammed shut just as he opened it. He recognized the foot that had hit the door.

"You're not leaving!" Nina's furious voice was right behind him. He swiveled to face her and wished

2

he hadn't. Her eyes still showed signs of arousal, but now they were interlaced with anger. The combination was lethal. What man would ever be able to resist a woman who looked at him that way?

"Go back home, Nina." He tamped down his urge to grab her.

"That's all you've got to say?" He saw the hurt in her face.

"You should stay away from me." He was no good for her. Eventually he would hurt her, and it would be worse than what she felt now. If he were smart, he would wipe her memory of him right now and be done with it. But all his smarts had deserted him for the night.

"You're rejecting me, after the way you touched me?"

"That's right." His throat felt tight, and he couldn't breathe.

"Fine. Go, leave. I don't need you. There are plenty of men in this city who'll take what I'm offering. And what do I care who it is? As long as he's got a big dick, there's no difference to me anyway! Somebody will finish what you've started." Nina turned on her heels.

Had he heard right? Another man? She was going to sleep with *another man*?

Amaury snatched her by her jacket and pulled her back to face him. She was going to let another man touch her, kiss her, make love to her? Over his fucking dead body!

"Get in the damn car!"

She shot him a surprised look.

"Now!" Before he lost it and took her against the car door to assert his claim.

The moment they both sat in the car, he stepped on the gas and shot into the street. He was reeling. She'd manipulated him, pushed his buttons. The little vixen had made him jealous! Him, the man who couldn't care less about women unless it was to scratch an itch.

A warm hand slipped onto his thigh, and he let out a low growl. "You don't know what you're getting into."

Nina leaned into him, which wasn't difficult considering how small the inside of his Porsche Carrera was. "Neither do you."

Her hand traveled higher up his thigh, playing havoc with his concentration. He sped up and ran a red light. Angry honking behind him followed, but he ignored it.

"You're playing a dangerous game." His warning seemed to go right over her head as her palm suddenly cupped the bulge in his pants. Had there been any space in the car, he would have leapt out of his seat, but all he could do was let out a frustrated moan. "Are you trying to make me crash the car?"

"I just want to make sure you won't change your mind again."

Amaury shot her a sideways glance. "I can make you a promise right now. You won't get away from me until I've fucked you every which way I can think of, and then some. And then I'll do it all over again, because you'll beg me to."

He didn't care that he sounded arrogant. He didn't care about anything at this point. All he wanted was to be inside her. Only then would he be able to think clearly again. Right, that was what he needed. He was sure afterwards things would go back to normal for him.

Her warm palm squeezed his erection as if in agreement, and he let out a stifled groan.

"Damn it, Nina, can't you wait two minutes?"

"Drive faster if you don't want to get arrested for getting a blow job in the car."

His foot pressed the gas pedal in desperation, while he felt her nudging open the zipper of his pants. A block before his building her hand reached in to pull out his cock. He hit the garage door opener and increased the speed, gritting his teeth.

The Porsche shot into the large private garage with not a second to spare, the garage door already closing behind them. The instant he came to a stop and killed the engine, he pulled her hand off and yanked her toward him.

"You know what happens to naughty girls?"

Nina looked almost innocent when she shook her short blond curls, tickling his face with them. Her intoxicating scent wrapped around him. "No."

"They end up with real bad boys."

A flicker of excitement illuminated her eyes. "Like you?"

"Like me." She had no idea what she was getting into and neither did he.

"Are you still angry with me?"

"Yes." But he would redirect his anger and turn it into passion instead.

"Do you want to spank me again?"

He raised an eyebrow. She sounded just a little too eager. What the hell had he started? What if he couldn't handle her? Or was she just what he needed? "I'll think about it."

Amaury gazed at her red lips which beckoned for

a kiss. "Let's go upstairs. This car is not conducive to what I have in mind." Because one kiss would lead to much more, and he sure couldn't move in the damn car.

When he got out of the Porsche, he realized his cock was still peeking out of his pants. A cool breeze blew against his flesh. But he didn't bother adjusting himself. The garage was private and the elevator he had built in led directly into his apartment. None of the tenants had access to it.

As soon as he'd pulled Nina into the elevator and pushed the button to the top floor, he pressed her flat against the wall and sank his hungry lips onto hers.

He meant it when he said he wouldn't let her go until he'd thoroughly fucked her. And he wasn't going to waste another damn minute. The elevator was as good a place to start as any. The housekeeper had come by the day before, so he knew even the floor of the elevator was spotless, just in case he decided to make use of it. Maybe he would.

Amaury crushed her lips with his and dipped into her delicious mouth, searching out her talented tongue. Her response was hard and determined, drawing him into her tantalizing depths. Inviting him, pulling him in, then withdrawing so he would come after her. Playing not hard to get, but hard to keep. A challenge he only too gladly accepted.

He released a sigh and foraged deeper, barely able to breathe, yet unable to stop the kiss. She tasted too sweet, too innocent, when he knew she wasn't innocent, not by a long shot. Not the way she'd taken his cock into her mouth the night before or the way she kissed him now.

Nina's hands eagerly tugged at his jacket, pushing

it off his shoulders with ease. She seemed to like undressing him, and he welcomed it since his body was heating up fast. The eight-by-four-foot space would turn into a sauna shortly, given the body heat they were generating. Just as well, since he was planning on stripping her naked in seconds.

Amaury liberated her from the leather jacket she still wore, dropping it unceremoniously onto the clean floor. She wore a T-shirt underneath. When he pulled her against his chest, he felt her soft breasts mold to him without a bra impeding them. He appreciated the simplicity of her clothing, her no-frills style.

His hand found its way underneath her shirt, instantly relishing the softness and warmth of her skin. He let the moment sink in, enjoyed the first contact of skin on skin, before he allowed himself to move upwards, where her twin globes beckoned to be attended to.

His fingertips reached her first, touched the underside of her breast, then slid farther north, searching and then finding the hardened little bud which already stood erect as if greeting his arrival. So he returned the gesture by stroking his thumb over it, applying just enough pressure to elicit a soft moan from its owner. A moan he'd anticipated and now captured with his hungry mouth. A moan which now reverberated through his body, awakening cells long dormant, sensations long forgotten.

"Somebody will see us," Nina whispered against his lips. He curled the ends of his mouth upwards. Her concern was unwarranted, but she couldn't know that, and he wouldn't tell her. She seemed like the kind of woman who would like the added risk of being discovered. And he wanted her just as horny as he was right now.

"So what? I promise you, I won't let anybody join in." Not that he had any objections to threesomes, but when it came to Nina, he didn't want to share her. This was just between the two of them. Private. Intimate.

He pushed her T-shirt up. "Take it off, Nina."

"Make me."

She wanted to play? He growled low and dark, then tugged at it with his teeth. One pull and the shirt ripped, gaping open in the middle.

"You're bad." Her voice was breathless, but not accusing.

"I haven't started yet."

Amaury reached for her beautiful round breasts, taking them into his hands, letting their weight be supported by his palms. As he squeezed lightly, he saw her lashes drop to half mast, partially hiding the desire in her eyes. Her gaze locked with his. Again he kneaded the soft flesh in his hands, and she reacted by pulling her lower lip between her teeth.

His cock tilted toward her, and he did himself a favor and pressed his groin against her sex. She answered by slinging her arms around his neck and pulling his face to her.

"Kiss me like you mean it." It was her demand, not his. Her wish, her choice.

Amaury's hand snaked around her back, while the other one slid to the back of her neck. He took her mouth hard and without mercy, forcing her lips open, driving his tongue into her like the spear of an ancient warrior, and he conquered. There was no resistance. She was his.

With one hand he jerked the button of her jeans

open, then pulled the zipper down. Like a mirror image she did the same to him. He needed both his hands to nudge her tight jeans down her hips.

"Help me."

Her hands joined in, and seconds later her pants fell to the ground. His own followed moments later and were instantly followed by his shirt and the torn rags which used to be her T-shirt. He didn't have the patience to let her take off her panties, so he ripped them off her. He'd buy her new ones. Actually, on second thought, he would make sure she'd never again wear any underwear.

Naked, they stood in front of each other. The elevator had long since stopped on the top floor, but the door hadn't opened. It would only do so if he used his key which was buried somewhere in the pile of clothes on the floor.

Amaury's gaze swept over her nude form. She was a real blonde, evidenced by the soft blond curls guarding her sex. Without a word he dropped to his knees and buried his face in her thatch of hair, taking in her scent. His tongue darted out, taking its first taste. One lap was confirmation enough that he'd be lost. Her juices coated his tongue and spread in his mouth. His nostrils flared, his fangs itched. She was more delicious than any dish he remembered from the time when he was human. And tastier than any blood he'd ever tasted, except for hers. He let out a deep sigh and dug his hands into her backside to pull her closer to him.

Nina's breathing appeared more uneven now, and his sensitive hearing picked up her rapid heartbeat. He looked up and found her watching him.

"Come down here." He pulled her to the floor

with him and placed her flat down before him, spreading her over the clothes. With deliberate movements he opened her legs and let his eyes devour her where his mouth would follow.

Her pink folds glistened with her desire, teasing his senses. Amaury sank his mouth onto her and explored her most intimate center. He realized instantly that he'd been wrong—his life would never go back to normal again, not after a night of passion in her arms.

2

Yvette's Haven

Scanguards Vampires

NEW YORK TIMES BESTSELLING AUTHOR

TINA FOLSOM

Haven tried to calm his galloping heart. Holding Yvette in his arms helped a little, reassuring him that she was alive and well. Had he not watched her while he'd been listening to his sister's stories, he wouldn't have picked up quickly enough that something was wrong. But the instant he'd seen her scan the room for danger, his own senses had picked up the sound and realized what it was.

He'd never moved that quickly in his entire life. He'd acted on pure instinct when he'd grabbed her and practically slammed her into the tiny bathroom to get her out of the way before Bess had pried a corner of the plywood away from the window. He still felt his knees tremble at the thought. But he was in no mood to examine his reaction to the threat that was solely aimed at Yvette. He didn't want to dig too deeply into his reasons for why he was protecting her.

He didn't want to think right now. He only wanted to feel. Her.

Haven eased up on his tight hold and shelved her chin on his hand, tilting her face up to him. The shock and fear in her eyes had dissipated. In its place was surprise.

"Kiss me," he demanded.

And damn it if she didn't move her head closer to his to follow his command without objection. He'd at least expected a little tussle before she'd give in. But maybe she was just as shocked as he was and needed this release as much as he needed it.

"But this time, don't bite me. I want to make sure that what I feel has nothing to do with any side effects." Not that he hadn't enjoyed her bite, but he was desperate to find out why he was so drawn to her. And the only way to figure it out was if she didn't use any of her vampire powers on him. He needed to be sure.

"No biting," she whispered on a shallow breath. "Not even a little?"

His cock hardened at the mere suggestion. Haven shut his eyes for a moment, trying to block her out.

Instead, the darkness only intensified Yvette's presence. Her orange scent was all around him, the sound of her heartbeat reverberating against his chest, and her shallow breaths blew warm air against his face. Her hands now moved up his chest, the skin-on-skin contact sending electric shocks of lust through his veins as they traced their way toward his shoulders.

This woman would be his death if he allowed her to get too close.

"No," he finally answered before he opened his eyes and looked into hers. Deep down in those green eyes lay the answers to all his questions. "No, baby, right now, this is just between you and me. No tricks, no powers."

Just plain lust.

Raw.

Untamed.

When her lips met his, he forgot everything that had just happened. Only the sensation of soft lips pressing against him registered in his mind: sinful lips that knew what to do, passionate lips that explored them. Haven parted his lips, and invited her. How he loved the feel of a confident woman who simply took what she wanted. Just as much as he liked to take from her. To drink from her lips, to explore her, to make her respond to him.

When her tongue ran along his lower lip in a sensual caress so soft, a softness of which he'd never thought a vampire capable, he growled in frustration. He couldn't deal with soft right now. Didn't she understand that? He needed fast, hard, pounding. Only then would the shock of almost losing her be wiped away.

But her seductive tongue continued its teasing and only slowly dipped between the seam of his lips. When her taste filled his mouth, he inhaled deeply, taking in her enticing flavors. They hit a nerve inside him, telling his body to prepare for the inevitable. His heart pumped more blood into his cock, bringing his impatient friend near to bursting.

But it seemed Yvette wasn't done with her tender explorations and pressed herself closer to him, angling her head for deeper penetration now. Her body was warm, hot even, and at every spot her body connected with his, passion started its low boil, its slow ascent toward a peak still far in the distance.

Unable to content himself with the slow build, he turned with her in his arms and pressed her against the door, pinning her. The door moaned its protest, but Haven barely heard it. With single-minded determination, he forged his tongue into her mouth and hijacked the kiss. So much for asking *her* to kiss *him*. He wouldn't make that mistake again until they truly had time for this. At present, they didn't. Because he hadn't forgotten where they were. At any time, the witch could intrude, and he needed to get inside Yvette and still his hunger for her before that happened.

Yvette responded instantly to his passionate kiss, stroking her tongue against his, showing him she wouldn't be outdone. Now she was talking. He groaned his approval and lifted his head for a second. "There you go, baby."

An instant later, his lips went back to devour her, his tongue diving deep into her, tasting her, exploring her, at the same time as his hips ground against her. His cock directed his rhythm as it slid against her soft center, moving himself up and down. When her hand slipped to the waistband of his pants, he let out a ragged breath and ripped his mouth from hers.

"Take me out, Yvette."

Her hand went to his button, easing it open, before she went for his zipper.

"You can come out now," Wesley's voice came through the door.

Shit!

He couldn't go out there right now—because Yvette had just taken his cock out of its confinement, her palm resting around him as she too had her head turned toward Wesley's voice.

"Give us a few minutes." He sure hoped his brother would go away and leave him alone.

Haven listened. There was no reply to his request. Good. Then he looked back at Yvette who gave him a questioning look, before she dropped her gaze down to where she was still holding his cock.

A moment later, she stroked him in her fist. He nearly jumped out of his skin at the intense pleasure. "Fuck, baby!" he moaned under his breath.

His hands hiked up her dress which had already ridden up. Now it bunched at her hips, revealing her black g-string. Pushing the fabric aside with one hand, he slipped a finger along her folds, following its path downwards. Her curls were damp, but it was nothing compared to the dew her pussy was drenched in.

Without any resistance, his finger slipped between her folds and drove into her warm slit. Yvette's head dropped back against the door as she let out a breath.

"That's right, baby. That's where I want my cock. Right now. Spread your legs for me." Looking at him from under her lowered lashes, she widened her

15

stance.

Haven pulled his finger out and gripped her hips, lifting her up so her legs spread around his hips, using the door at her back as leverage. Then it hit him.

"Shit, I've got no condom."

She shook her head. "Vampires don't carry disease."

He'd figured as much, but it wasn't what he was worried about. "What about birth control?" The last thing he wanted was to have a child, another person to worry about like he'd worried about his sister. He didn't think he could go through this again. No, it would be better if he never had children who he would be afraid of losing.

When he looked into her eyes, he saw a strange glint there, but he couldn't figure out what it was. "You okay?"

"You won't have to worry about a pregnancy."

Haven liked a woman who took precautions. He dipped his head to her collarbone and nibbled along her skin. God, she smelled good. Good enough to eat. Later, when they had more time, he would learn her entire body with his lips, explore her, taste her, but right now, he needed something else. "Guide me inside."

Using one hand, she pushed her g-string to the side, then positioned his cock at her entrance. The moment she let go and wrapped her arms and legs around him, he plunged inside, the impact of it slamming them both against the door. The rattling of the door's hinges echoed in the small room.

"What are you doing in there?" Wesley's voice penetrated, this time accompanied by a hard knock on the door.

"Go away," Haven yelled back and withdrew from Yvette's sheath only to plunge deeper with his second thrust. Fuck, she was tight.

"If you're not coming out, I'm coming in there!" Wesley's threat made him stop for a second and stare at Yvette.

"Your choice," Yvette said in a low voice only for him to hear. "But if you stop now, there's no guarantee you'll ever get another chance at fucking me." Despite her nonchalant look, Haven knew she wasn't indifferent about the outcome of their little tryst. She wanted this to continue just as much as he did, and she wasn't fooling him or anybody else.

He *tsk*ed. "I've made you spread your legs once, I can do it again," he teased. Her reaction to him had been so passionate, he'd never been so certain in his life that they would continue what they'd started.

Suddenly she pushed against him, his cock dislodging in the process. Her eyes narrowed, and she dropped her legs to the floor before pushing him away from her in earnest. "You arrogant prick! I spread my legs when I want to, not when you decide it."

She tugged on her dress, letting it fall down her thighs. "We're coming out," she yelled toward the door and turned away from him, reaching for the handle.

"No, we're not!" Haven's hand slammed against the door, just as Yvette had turned the handle.

Her furious glare hit him as she pivoted to face him. "You can't keep me in here against my will!"

Haven took one step and pressed her back against the door once more. "Can't I?"

Before she could answer, he captured her lips and

kissed her. This time, there was nothing gentle about the kiss, nothing tentative. He'd establish right now that she wasn't going to escape him.

~ ~ ~

Screw him! Damn Haven that he could make her body turn traitor even when she was mad at him. And she was hopping mad. The arrogant prick thought just because she'd allowed him inside her, he was suddenly in charge. As if he believed himself superior. Like she was simply the weak woman, who'd submit as soon as the big bad bounty hunter and vampire slayer willed it so. Who did he think he was? He had no right to demand anything of her—and she alone would decide if he could fuck her later or not. Haven was not the boss of her.

Unfortunately, he was doing a pretty good job with kissing her into submission. But she wouldn't let him get the upper hand. She would fight with everything she had. She couldn't allow him to have any power over her, because she knew how things like that ended. Particularly in their case: Haven already had a low opinion of her, and his callous words that he could make her spread her legs for him whenever he wanted only confirmed that he had no respect for her. He would use her and then toss her aside like a used candy wrapper. But she wouldn't allow it. No, *she* would be the one tossing *him* aside when the time came, but not until she'd made him completely and utterly besotted with her. Payback was a bitch, and Yvette knew a lot about bitches.

There was only one way to achieve her goal of turning the tables on him: give him ultimate ecstasy and make him hunger for more, then deny him what he wanted most. He wasn't the first man she'd turned into putty in her hands, and he wouldn't be the last.

Ripping her mouth from his, she pulled out of his embrace. His eyes were dark with desire, his lips full and moist. When she dropped her gaze to his groin, she saw his magnificent cock still standing erect. With vampire speed she grabbed his shoulders, turned him and pressed him against the door. Starting now, she'd be in charge.

"What the—"

But Yvette didn't give him a chance to finish his sentence. Instead she dropped to her knees, bringing her mouth level with his cock. A glance up at Haven's face brought her in contact with his surprise, which in an instant turned to red hot desire.

"Yeah, baby," he whispered.

Yvette took his heavy shaft into her palm and stroked along its smooth underside, before she guided it to her mouth and licked over the purple head. Pre-cum had already oozed from him, and she lapped up the salty drops, flattening her tongue over the slit, pressing gently.

Haven's head dropped back against the door as he hissed out a low breath. Yvette let a smile curve her lips. It wouldn't take much to make him pussy-whipped. Her only problem now was how she'd stop herself from enjoying this so much. Because licking pre-cum off him was making her womb clench with desire.

Yvette gripped his cock by the root and, forming a perfect O with her lips, she slid down on him to take him into her mouth. He was big, his erection instantly hitting the back of her throat. She relaxed her muscles, trying not to gag and pulled back an inch until she felt Haven's hands on her head.

With light pressure, Haven thrust back into her mouth, his movement accompanied by a deep groan. Several shallow breaths followed as if he was trying to steady himself, but Yvette knew better than to allow him to adjust to the sensations she caused in him. He'd get no reprieve. Using her other hand, she reached for his balls and cradled them, then scraped her fingernails against the sac. It instantly tightened, pulling its rounded contents up toward the root of his thrusting shaft.

She used her tongue and lips to suck him hard, to create a pressure she knew he couldn't withstand for long. And all the while, she enjoyed his taste and the texture of his beautiful flesh. She'd always liked sucking cock because it gave her power over a man and with Haven even more so. His moans and irregular breaths were indication enough that he was nearing the edge of his control. And making him lose control was something she wanted to experience.

Yvette inhaled deeply, allowing his male scent to flood her senses. It reached every cell in her body, making her desire for him almost unbearable. But it wasn't for her own pleasure that she did this; it was for his, so he would go mad with desire for her. Because only if she snapped his control could she hope to gain her own senses back and make him lose the hold he had over her. But hell, if she didn't enjoy every single second of this. It was impossible to tell her body not to react to him.

Haven's hard length pumped faster and faster, and she sucked harder.

"Oh, God!" he grunted.

His cock jerked, his orgasm imminent. Yvette's fangs lengthened, and she took his cock as deep as she could before she set her fangs at the base of it and broke through his skin.

"Fuck!" Haven's surprised grunt barely registered as his blood and cum mixed in her mouth. The combined taste of it sent a bolt of electrical charge into her clit, making her climax instantly.

Yvette relished the sensations traveling through her heated body while she continued sucking his blood and his semen from his cock, which continued pulsating in her mouth.

When she noticed him going slack against the door, she dislodged her fangs and let his shaft slip from her mouth, catching him as his back slid along the door, bringing him to a sitting position. His eyes were closed, but his hands were still on her head, pulling her against him now.

"I've never—" he broke off, taking a deep breath into his lungs. "This was—" Again, he didn't finish his sentence.

Yvette smiled, feeling almost languid from her powerful orgasm—and he hadn't even touched her. She could only imagine what it would be like when he did. But for now, she basked in the fruits of her labor: he was succumbing to her.

"You—" Haven opened his eyes, his gaze falling onto his cock that now lay flaccid against the dark nest of curls. There were remnants of blood at the base, even though the little puncture wounds were disappearing before his eyes. "You bit me!"

3

Portia glanced in the mirror. Her low-rider jeans showed off her flat stomach, and the T-shirt was at least a size too small and short enough to leave her midriff bare while it stretched tightly over her boobs. She had to admit that Lauren was right: she had decent boobs, full and round, and actually a little more shapely than most of her fellow students.

As a hybrid, she had developed faster during her teens, and her body was more mature than that of a nearly twenty-one-year-old human. Just as well: it would be dreadful to be stuck with a gangly teenage body for the rest of her life. But the body she had now, she could work with.

One way or another, Zane would give in to her. Even if she had to throw herself at him. She had five weeks left, and during those five weeks she would chisel away his resistance. No man could be that stoic and say no to something that was dangled in front of his nose every single night, not even Zane. He would crack sooner or later. Did that make her just a tad desperate?

Portia blew out a big breath and planted her legs wider apart, placed her hands on her hips and tried a seductive look in the mirror. She cringed. Maybe she needed a little more practice with that look. It didn't appear quite right yet, unless Zane was turned on by a cheesy grin accompanied by some waggling eyebrows. Maybe some more lipstick, she mused, and twisted the cap off her latest acquisition. As she dabbed her lips with more of the blood-red color, she knew she couldn't stall any longer. The night wouldn't last forever, and eventually Zane would be gone to be replaced by Oliver again.

Her hands clammy, she turned the door handle and left her room. Her heart beat so loudly, she was sure Zane could hear it downstairs in the living room. Slowly, she walked down the stairs, her bare feet making barely any sound. Only the creaking of several steps echoed through the old house. When she reached the landing, she could tell from Zane's stiff posture sitting in an armchair that he'd already heard her.

"Hi."

He looked up briefly, muttering an indistinguishable greeting, and lowered his head again to read the magazine he was holding. Or pretend to read. His eyes didn't appear to move from left to right, but seemed to stare at some random spot on the page.

Zane wore what he always wore: tight-fitting jeans, a black long-sleeved shirt, and boots that looked like he could kick the shit out of someone with them. His leather coat hung over a chair near the entrance. And damn it if that simple outfit didn't make him look like sex-on-a-stick. Why Lauren insisted his bald head was unattractive, Portia didn't understand. She had, in fact, never seen anybody who carried the loss of hair off the way Zane did, with his 'take it or leave it' kind of attitude, as if he didn't give a shit what anybody thought of him. Maybe that's what she liked most about him.

Liked? That was too strong a word. She didn't really 'like' him—more like she had the hots for him—and that was a totally different cup of tea. 'Like' had nothing to do with it.

"Are you done looking?" Zane grunted.

Shit! She hated it when he called her on it like that. She could only hope that she hadn't been drooling.

"Not much to see; you're wearing too many clothes."

His head shot up, his narrowed eyes glaring at her. "That kind of talk is dangerous."

She took a few steps in his direction, easing

closer. "Afraid of me?" Surprised at her own boldness, her pulse beat faster and more erratic than before.

He scoffed. "Don't you have homework to do, baby girl?"

Annoyance kicked in, lending her courage. "If you think by calling me 'baby girl' you can fool yourself into thinking I'm not a grown woman, go ahead."

Zane's knuckles gripping the magazine turned white. She was clearly getting to him, just as she'd anticipated. Unfortunately, however, instead of turning him on, she was pissing him off. Perhaps she wasn't that good on the flirting front. And why would she be? She'd never felt the need to flirt with anyone before, so she'd never bothered.

"I don't care if you're a grown woman. How often do I have to repeat myself? I'm NOT INTERESTED in you!"

Shocked by his violent outburst, she swiveled on her heels and headed for the kitchen. "Liar," she mumbled to herself before she tore the door open and went for the fridge.

Well, that was going brilliantly! Lauren had warned her that a man like Zane wouldn't be swayed easily. After this disaster she had to check in with her friend to see how she should proceed now. Lauren had a lot more experience with men. She would come up with something to salvage the situation.

Portia grabbed a coke, needing the sugar and caffeine rush, and closed the fridge door.

A split second later, she found herself pressed against the cool stainless steel surface. Zane's face was inches from hers. The coke can dropped from her grip and landed on the floor, making a loud noise on the tiles.

His teeth clenched, Zane issued his warning, "Never call me a liar!"

Her chest heaved from the sudden effort of breathing, her boobs pressing against his lean body with each breath, her nipples chafing and reacting instantly. When she tilted her hips forward, one realization infused her with courage to speak: he was sporting an erection.

"I'd call you lover, but you give me no choice."

Zane closed his eyes, his nostrils flaring at the same moment. "I'll never be your lover," he countered, all anger drained from his toneless voice. "Go play with somebody else before you start something you can't handle."

He thought she couldn't handle him? He was wrong! She would prove it to him.

Abruptly, Zane released his hold on her, but before he could step back, she framed his face with her hands and pressed her lips to his.

"Don't," he whispered but didn't pull back.

Portia licked her tongue over the seam of his lips, urging him to surrender. A thrill charged through her body when Zane moved. His lips parted, and the next moment she felt herself sandwiched between the fridge door and his hard body.

Her hands dropped from his face to wrap around his neck, making sure he wouldn't change his mind.

"You'll regret this," he murmured against her lips.

"I won't."

"I know *I* will." But despite his contradicting comment, he stroked his tongue against her lips before he delved into her, capturing her mouth in a move indicating ultimate possession. He held her so tightly, not even with her hybrid strength would she have been able to escape him had she wanted to.

Zane kissed her as if he wanted to punish her, his tongue the whip that lashed her until she was raw, his lips the ties that bound her to him as his hands traveled over her torso in a frantic race to touch every inch before either of them had a change of mind.

Tasting the raw hunger in his kiss, the obvious desperation to possess and devour, Portia's heart recognized her own need: to give herself to this man, this vampire, and to surrender to her desires, desires she'd never felt before. Everything was new and unknown. How had she lived until now without knowing what a touch and a kiss could do, how it could consume a person like a wildfire consumed a forest, leaving nothing behind but a charred surface?

That's how she felt, her skin seared as if hot lava touched her instead of the sensual long fingers of the most enticing man—human or vampire—she'd ever met. And those fingers did things to her, incredible things, exciting things: their touch was poison and soothing medicine all at once, first stirring up her insides, then calming them.

Their rhythm matched her breath, the tremors inside her reaching earthquake levels. Wherever Zane's body connected with hers, she burned—and burned for more. Like an addict, she pulled him closer, moaning her approval and her surrender in one breath. Yet he didn't seem to understand, continuing to unleash his devastating sexual prowess onto her when he could have stripped her of her clothes already and be driving into her without preamble.

Portia ripped her lips from his. "Take me now."

Zane didn't listen. His response was a growl, a sound only an animal could make. His eyes were glowing a deep orange, and his breath rushed from his lungs. Without a response, he took her mouth again, continuing where he'd left off as if she'd never interrupted.

Trying to ease the ache between her thighs, Portia drew up one leg and wrapped it around his thigh, making him press closer. She felt the hard outline of his erection against her soft core and rubbed herself against him, trying to find relief.

A groan rumbled from his chest and reverberated against her ribcage. One of his hands went to her backside, hauling her fully against him, increasing the friction between their bodies.

She went on tip toes to feel his erection pressing lower where her clit throbbed in concert with her heartbeat. Her hands went to his ass, her nails digging into the jeans she wished he wasn't wearing.

All of a sudden, Zane lifted her, forcing her legs farther apart, compelling her to wrap them around his hips as he thrust against her.

The fridge behind her rattled, containers inside tumbling from the shelves. She didn't care. Every time he thrust, his cock hit that little bundle of nerves that was swollen and aching for release. All she could think of was for him not to stop, for this never to end.

"I need..." she whimpered against his lips, unable to control her body's reactions any longer.

A moment later, she felt his fangs grazing her lip, nipping slightly. Her nose detected blood, but her tongue would never taste it, because Zane licked her blood off her lips and swallowed it.

"Fuck!" he cursed and closed his eyes.

She didn't know what he meant, nor did she care. "More!" As her hips ground against him, his cock dragging over her clit with every movement, she pulled his head back to her.

Ding Dong! Ding Dong!

No, not now! She would ignore it. Portia pressed her lips onto Zane's, hoping he hadn't heard the sound in his lust-drugged state, but he pulled back. In the next instant, she stood on her own two feet again, feet that were shaking uncontrollably, her entire body trembling with need.

"No!" she protested. She reached for him, but he turned his back to her.

"Fuck!" she heard him curse under his breath as he stalked out of the kitchen without another word or a look.

4

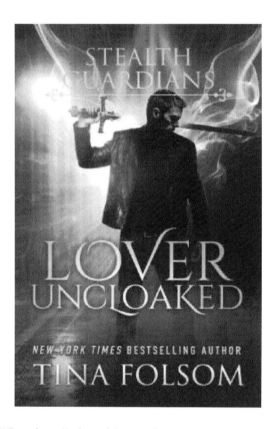

"Condom," she whispered.

He shook his head. "Immortals carry no disease."

"But I'm not on the pill."

Oddly enough, the fact that she wasn't using birth control pleased him, even though it didn't matter: only once bonded to a human could a Stealth

Guardian father children. In the meantime his sperm remained sterile.

"You won't get pregnant." As soon as he said it, a twinge of regret surged through him. Why did he suddenly wish that his seed would leave something lasting in her, when he'd never had this wish before? This could be nothing more than a fling, an affair that would last no longer than his assignment. To think of it as more was only inviting trouble. Yet at the same time, something in him revolted against the notion of leaving her.

"Are you sure?"

"I'm sure, Leila."

Gazing into the deep blue of her eyes, he nudged forward, his cock parting her outer lips, her moist heat coating his bulbous head. He clenched his jaw at the tightness of her muscles and slid farther inside.

His heart rate accelerated and all the air left his lungs. Then he felt her legs wrap around his hips, her heels digging into his backside. Knowing he couldn't hold off any longer, he plunged inside—into pure heaven.

Like a silken glove, she wrapped around him, her interior muscles velvety soft, yet gripping him firmly, her juices making him slide into her as if into liquid heat. His whole body burned from the intensity of the contact with Leila, his pulse beating violently under his skin. As blood raced through his veins, he moved inside her, withdrew, then thrust back in. First slowly, then with more determination.

Underneath him, she responded to his movements, arching her back, undulating her hips to urge him closer and deeper. As if, like him, she couldn't get enough of this new connection. And it felt like a connection, not just mindless copulating, but a connection of two bodies that seemed perfect for each other. His previous one-night-stands had been frantic fucks without much involvement, simply rides toward completion. This was different. His gaze locked with hers, he looked into her and recognized the desire and passion that burned there, the need for more waiting in the wings. He was unable to tear himself away from the sight and continued to revel in her inner beauty—beauty he could see shining beneath her pretty shell.

The strength he saw there was what made this all the more exciting. For the first time, he shared intimacies with a human whose strength he admired, whose determination he understood. And as her body took him inside her, trusting him not to hurt her, he felt the walls he'd build around himself crumble. As they did, he felt his entire body begin to shimmer in a silvery fog. It engulfed Leila with him.

The moment she seemed to notice this change in him, her eyes widened. "What's happening?" she gasped.

He brushed his lips against her mouth. "I'm making love to you the Stealth Guardian way." Something he'd never done before, never felt safe enough with anybody before. "Hold on, baby."

Allowing his energy to flow freely, the fog intensified, whirling around them like a storm. The room seemed to disappear and only their bodies remained, floating. Sparks of energy lit around them as he continued driving into her, his strokes hard and deep, increasing in speed and intensity as the fog grew thicker.

Sealing her lips with a kiss and intertwining his

tongue with hers, he held her tightly, his cock pounding into her soft flesh harder than any human woman could take. Yet he wouldn't hurt her, because as he made love to her, he shared his energy and strength with her, let her feel the essence of his power so she could taste ultimate ecstasy.

The pressure in his balls built and intensified to a point where he could hold back no longer. As his orgasm claimed him, his seed shot through his cock and into her body. With it, a spear of energy surged into her, the Stealth Guardian's virta, making her body shimmer in a golden light. In the same instant, she screamed out her release, her muscles contracting around him.

Slowly, they floated back down, the fog around them vanishing, and the room reappearing.

He looked down at her and into her stunned eyes.

"Oh, my God!" she whispered, then looked at her arms, inspecting them. "I'm glowing." She stared at him, a thousand questions reflecting in her eyes.

"Yes, and you'll glow for a few hours like that."

"What did you do to me?" There was no accusation in her voice, only curiosity.

"When a Stealth Guardian makes love the ancient way, his energy flows into his partner. It will stay there for hours after lovemaking."

"Why?"

"Because of this." He grinned and shifted, pulling his cock back and then plunging back inside. A gasp was her answer as her eyelids fluttered and shudders went through her sensitive body. "As long as you glow, the slightest touch by me will give you another orgasm. A Stealth Guardian takes care of his woman."

"I'll never survive this," she said in disbelief.

He laughed out loud and threw his head back. "You will, Leila, because while you glow you're nearly as strong as I am." He paused and winked mischievously. "And nearly as insatiable."

"So there is an ulterior motive to this glowing trick. You want to make sure your women don't get tired of sex."

"Well, I did mention earlier that I was selfish, did I not?"

She smiled back at him and licked her lips, her pink tongue so enticing that he felt more blood rush to his cock. "What happens when you make a woman glow who's already insatiable to begin with?"

His heart made a somersault at her seductive remark. "It makes for a very, very wild night. Without sleep, without rest, and without regret."

Leila batted her eyelashes at him and slid her hand behind his head, pulling him to her. "Then let's see if I'm really almost as strong as you."

Before he knew what she was planning to do, she'd flipped him on his back and was on top of him.

He smirked. "Maybe I should have thought twice about making you glow."

Slowly she began to ride him, moving up and down on his shaft, her muscles squeezing him harder now than before, an effect of the power he'd poured into her.

"Or maybe not," he conceded and pulled her head to him for a kiss. "Ride me, my beautiful Leila."

~ ~ ~

Leila felt amazing, free, powerful, and above all fearless. All of a sudden, all her fear had dissipated, dissolved into nothing, into meaningless thoughts that had no place in her body now—a body that felt reenergized and elevated, lifted from its ordinary life to something so different, she had a hard time putting it into words.

When Aiden had come inside of her and her entire body had all of a sudden started to glow, she'd felt an instant surge of power inside her, making her feel as if she could run a marathon and win it. But that wasn't even the most amazing thing about it. More importantly, she'd suddenly seen a tiny glimpse of his soul, of the vulnerable man inside. It had been so fleeting that she'd dismissed it as impossible. Yet when he'd explained to her that he'd shared his power with her, she'd realized that he must have shared more—even more than he thought he had.

That knowledge wiped out her mistrust in him. And at the same time, it brought forward the guilt about what she was still hiding from him. Even now, as she was on top of him, impaled on his rock-hard cock, the pendant that contained the last copy of her research data hung around her neck. It felt as if it burned there against her flesh, urging her to tell him the truth. To confess.

But at the same time she remembered what he'd said to her earlier, that all her data must be destroyed. For the sake of her parents, she couldn't let it happen. She had to hold onto the hope that maybe soon he'd understand, that maybe after a night in each other's arms they would grow closer. Then she could ask him to reconsider, to help her find a way to keep her research alive.

Tomorrow, she promised herself, *tomorrow I'll tell him*.

Tonight was meant for lovemaking and nothing else. Her body was primed for it, her own desire for him, coupled with his power inside her, making for an intoxicating cocktail of sensations. Sensations she couldn't and wouldn't deny herself now. The lust raging in her was too strong to hold back.

"How do you want it?" she whispered against his lips.

"Surprise me."

Then his hands went to her hips, gripping them. With one forceful move, he slammed her down onto him, driving his cock into her to the hilt, sending another wave of ecstasy through her body.

"And do it soon, or I'll take over," he warned between clenched teeth. "Because every time you come while I'm connected to you, you drive me to the edge."

Taking his hands by the wrists, she pried them off her hips and pinned them next to his head, leaning over him, her breasts dangling close to his face. Slowly, she gyrated her hips, letting his cock slide in and out.

"If you want to come, then you'll have to do something for it." She lowered her lids to indicate her breasts.

"Nothing easier than that," he agreed and lifted his head, wrapping his lips around one nipple.

As he sucked it into his mouth and licked his tongue over it, waves of pleasure rocked through her body once more. Of their own volition, her hips started to move in a rhythm as old as time, and she rode him the way the waves dictated to her. As in an African mating dance, she let her body take over, move in synch with his, giving and taking all at once.

She heard moans fill the room, his and her own, and listened to the sounds of flesh slapping together.

The scent of sex permeated the air around them, and the dim bedside lamp created a tableau of light and shadows that danced on their skin.

Beneath her, Aiden sucked greedily at her breasts, licked and tortured her nipples that had long ago turned into hard points so sensitive a light breeze could ignite them. Inside her, an inferno was raging that felt hotter than the fires of hell could possibly be.

And all the while, she rode his marble hard shaft, bringing him to the edge of his release again and again. With each of her orgasms, he screamed out in pure passion, and thrust deeper into her.

"Now," he urged, his body bathed in sweat. "Give me everything."

Instinct that could only come from Aiden's power made her place her hand over his heart as she threw her head back and only concentrated on him and how much she wanted to feel his release.

A sudden warmth flooded her, and she felt it run down her shoulder to her arm, into her elbow and lower still.

Before it could reach her fingertips and connect with his skin, she felt her hand ripped from his chest. She snapped her head toward Aiden, noticing a shocked expression on his face.

A second later, she felt him explode inside her, harder than the first time.

She collapsed onto him and felt his arms wrap around her as his body trembled from the aftershocks of his orgasm.

"How did you know?" he asked, his voice hoarse.

But before she could form a word, darkness claimed her.

5

Thomas stood in the shower and let the warm water run down his body as if it could wash away his worries. Another night had passed without any sign of the four vampires who'd killed Sergio and his mate. And while he knew intellectually that he couldn't have prevented this tragedy, in his heart he felt responsible.

He tried to put the thoughts out of his mind, but that only meant that other thoughts pushed to the forefront. Thoughts about Eddie. He hadn't seen him all night, and after checking the staff roster, he'd realized that Eddie had taken a vacation day. Samson himself had authorized it. Strange, neither Eddie nor Samson had mentioned anything to him. And Eddie had left on his motorcycle as soon as the sun had set.

Thomas reached for the soap and lathered up, cleaning the grease from his body after he'd tinkered with one of his motorcycles for a few hours. It had helped him focus. He had to do something. Sitting around and waiting for the next atrocity to happen was not an option. Tomorrow night, he would go out and search for Xander, the man who'd asked him to join Kasper's disciples. He would use him to ferret out the others and then figure out how to destroy them.

Feeling better about having formulated a plan, he rinsed the soap off his body and turned off the water. There was silence now, but it was interrupted by the even breathing of a man other than himself. He inhaled and recognized the scent.

"Leave!" he ordered and continued to stare at the tiles that lined his oversized shower stall.

But no sound of footsteps followed his command.

"Eddie, get out now! You can't be in here. I don't have the strength to suppress my desire for you, not today. You're better off locking yourself in your room. Leave! Please leave!"

He braced one hand against the tile wall, steadying himself while his body betrayed him, his cock pumping full with blood, making it rise like a

Phoenix. There was no way he could turn around now. It was bad enough that Eddie could see his naked backside. Showing him his erection and admitting that he was powerless in his presence would only make things worse.

When he heard bare feet on the floor, he almost let out a sigh of relief—until he realized that they were coming closer instead of moving away. He closed his eyes and clenched his jaw, fighting against the urge to turn around and pull Eddie into the shower with him.

"You have to leave," he begged once more, but it was too late.

Eddie's hand touched his shoulder, turning him around to face him. Eddie's brown eyes looked straight at him, connecting with his gaze, before they wandered down his body, stopping at the place, where Thomas's cock stood erect.

Thomas's heart stopped beating as he let his gaze travel over Eddie's body. His chest was bare. Tight abs flexed just above his low-riding pajama pants. The thin material tented at Eddie's groin. Thomas's throat went dry. He was unable to swallow.

Nor was he able to move when Eddie's hand stroked over his chest, grazing his nipple and turning it rock hard in an instant. But Eddie's hand didn't remain on his chest. It dove lower, went past his navel, and reached the thatch of hair that guarded Thomas's sex. When his fingers combed through the coarse hair, Thomas held his breath, afraid of breaking the spell. At the first contact of Eddie's hand with his cock, Thomas let out an involuntary groan. Then his breathing went into overdrive.

Eddie's hand wrapped around him, the warm skin

of his palm covering him like a blanket.

"Fuck!" Thomas hissed under his breath.

Eddie's eyes shot up to meet his gaze. His lips moved. "You like that?" His pink tongue licked his lips, making Thomas let out another sound of pleasure. Was he dreaming? Because this couldn't be happening. Why was Eddie suddenly in his shower, touching him when only two nights ago, he'd made it clear that the kiss at the construction site had been merely a diversionary tactic? What had changed Eddie's mind?

Eddie tightened his grip around Thomas's hard-on, then slid up and down on it. "If we do this, you have to promise me something," he demanded.

"Anything," Thomas replied without thinking, since his brain had already shut down and his dick was doing his thinking for him now.

"Nobody can ever find out."

"Nobody," he whispered back, his breath deserting him as Eddie moved closer.

"Undress me."

Thomas reached for the strings that held up Eddie's pajama pants and untied them with trembling fingers. When the knot was open, he loosened the waistband and pushed the pants past Eddie's slim hips. From there, they fell onto the wet shower floor, pooling around Eddie's feet.

Thomas dropped his gaze and stared at Eddie's cock. It was fully erect and more beautiful than anything he'd ever seen. Pumped full with blood, plump veins snaked around the shaft, its purple head glistening with pre-cum. He took a deep breath, inhaling the tantalizing scent, sending a shockwave through his body.

"Eddie," he murmured, unable to form a coherent sentence.

Instead, he slipped his hand between Eddie's legs and palmed his balls, then gripped his erection. Eddie's breath hitched, and for a moment, his hand on Thomas's cock stilled in its movements.

Eddie let go of Thomas's cock, then laid his hand over Thomas's and pried it off him. Disappointed, Thomas stared at him.

"Together," Eddie whispered and pushed his cock against Thomas's, then put his hand around both cocks at the same time, though his palm couldn't span the combined girth fully.

Thomas added his hand, and together they moved their hands up and down their joined erections. Feeling the soft skin of Eddie's cock against his own hard-on, Thomas felt overwhelmed by the sensations racing through his body: fire shot through his cells, electricity fueled the flames in his body, desire surged.

Eddie let out a ragged breath, his lids lowering. Thomas slanted his head and brought his lips to Eddie's, brushing against them. A moan left Eddie's throat and Thomas captured it, closing his lips over Eddie's mouth.

The moment their tongues met, pleasure so intense he thought it would kill him rushed through him. He'd dreamed of this so many times, spent so many days in his bed imagining how it would feel. But now that it was happening, now that he and Eddie were making love, he realized that his fantasies had been pale copies in comparison to what he was experiencing now.

Eddie's hand stroking him, his tongue dueling with him, his thighs pressing against him, made his pulse race. And if vampires could suffer heart attacks, Thomas would surely die from one. Sliding his free hand onto Eddie's ass, he ground against him, making him aware of his unquenchable desire for him.

Eddie's hand started moving at a faster tempo as he slid up and down their cocks. Thomas matched his strokes to Eddie's, feeling his excitement rise along with his own.

Thomas intensified the kiss, sucking, stroking, exploring his lover with more fervor, diving deeper into the sweet caverns of his mouth, nibbling on his lips, then licking his tongue over them.

When Eddie's head fell back, severing the kiss, Thomas kissed the tempting column of his neck, his lips latching onto the plump vein that pulsed there. He could sense the blood rushing through the vein, the pulsing sensation that indicated the heartbeat, just as he could smell the blood. It called to him like a beacon that guided a lost soul to shore. Taking a lover's blood was part of what many vampires did during the sex act. It heightened their arousal and intensified their coupling. Temptation roared through Thomas as his fangs extended and brushed against Eddie's hot skin.

~ ~ ~

Eddie felt Thomas's mouth on his neck and his sharp teeth sliding along his skin. The sensation sent a spear of heat through his core and right into his cock. He'd never felt anything better in his life, and all they were doing was rubbing their cocks together, their hands joined, their rhythms in perfect harmony.

Maybe this was the way to get this out of his system. At least that's what he'd thought at first when he'd walked into Thomas's bathroom. Just one quick fuck and he would realize that this wasn't what he wanted, and then he'd finally kill his desire for Thomas and get back to being his friend. Unfortunately, the moment he'd touched Thomas and wrapped his hand around his magnificent cock, he'd realized that it wouldn't be so easy. Maybe they would have to fuck more than once for Eddie to satisfy his *gay tendencies*.

Eddie's free hand wandered over Thomas's body, exploring the hard ridges on his abdomen and the smooth, hairless skin that covered his chest. Then he roamed his back, sliding down to the curve where his firm ass waited. His cheeks clenched as Eddie palmed him, and a corresponding moan rolled over Thomas's lips. He felt Thomas's hand tighten over his ass and tried to suppress his reaction to it, but a sigh left his lips nevertheless. The possessive touch did something to him, urging him to react to the call of his lover like animals answered the mating calls of their mates.

Thomas's hips pumped, thrusting his cock harder and faster as his hand tightened over Eddie's hand, pushing their cocks harder together. Already now, he could feel the moisture that was lubricating them. Whose cock it had seeped from, Eddie couldn't tell for certain. Probably from both.

"I'm coming," Thomas ground out, his breath labored. He lifted his head from Eddie's neck. "Can't hold it back."

Eddie let go of the control with which he'd held himself back, and thrust harder. "Yes!" he cried out, proud of the fact that he could bring a strong vampire like Thomas to lose control just by pumping his cock in his hand. "Come," he urged him and captured his lips with a passionate kiss.

Then he felt wetness spread between his fingers, and a loud groan come from Thomas's chest. The pleasure of feeling Thomas surrender in his arms did him in: hot semen shot through his cock and exploded from the tip, raining over his and Thomas's hands as they continued to stroke each other more slowly now. His body shook with pleasure, his knees going weak at the same time. He ripped his lips from Thomas's mouth, trying to catch his breath, when he felt Thomas's free arm wrap around his waist, catching him before his knees could buckle.

"I've got you," Thomas murmured, pressing his forehead against Eddie's.

Eddie closed his eyes, unable to return Thomas's gaze. He'd just made love to a man, and fuck, he'd liked it. What did that make him? He didn't want to answer that question. He wasn't ready for the answer. Besides, all they'd done was masturbate together. Didn't guys do that in college all the time?

Right, a sarcastic voice in his head answered. *And they probably touch each other's cocks all the time.*

Eddie pushed away the thought when he felt warm water run down his body and Thomas's hands gently cleaning him. Without thinking he leaned into him.

"I loved it," Thomas said.

Eddie couldn't bring himself to reciprocate the words, even though deep inside, he knew he felt the same. Instead he buried his head in the crook of Thomas's neck.

He felt Thomas reach for the towel that hung just outside the shower and put it around Eddie's back, patting him dry. Eddie let it happen as if he were a helpless child. He was unable to sever the contact with Thomas's body and realized that it was because he was hungry, hungry for more. This... *episode* had only whet his appetite.

6

NEW YORK TIMES BESTSELLING AUTHOR
TINA FOLSOM
A SCENT OF GREEK
Out of Olympus

Dio cast Ariadne another glance. Something was off. Whenever he asked her about his past, she got nervous. Was there something in his past she didn't want to share with him? The thought made unease slither down his back like a snake. Perhaps it was better if he tried to figure things out on his own.

Later, he'd continue scouting out the addresses he'd found in his apartment in the hope that some speck of memory returned. But while he was with Ariadne, he might as well use the time to get closer to her. Since he'd bent to her will to deal with his so-called drinking problem, it was time that *she* did something *he* wanted. Quid pro quo.

When Ariadne suddenly stopped in front of a shop, Dio looked up at the sign above the door. *In Vino Veritas* it said. His mind instantly translated the words for him: truth in wine. He spoke Latin, but he also realized that it wasn't his native language. Neither was English. He was definitely educated—classically educated, evidently.

Dio followed her into the shop and closed the door, leaving the sounds of the traffic behind him. Hundreds of bottles neatly stacked on various racks and display cases reached out to him to greet him like the prodigal son. A welcoming surge of recognition washed over him and wrapped around him like a warm towel after a cold shower.

His eyes traveled over the bottles, caressing their contents through the dark glass that contained the precious liquid. He felt relaxed and content for the first time since the onset of his amnesia. The wine bottles spoke to him almost in deference, as if they were his subjects and he their king. Dio shook his head at the stupid notion. Clearly, the AA meeting had scrambled his brain. There was no way he was going back there.

He'd never felt so uncomfortable in his life—or the little of his life that he remembered. The thought of giving up wine for good was unfathomable to him. Why would anybody do such a thing? Wine was life, fun, and even healthy for that matter. And besides, why would Ariadne want him to give up drinking when she owned a wine shop herself? No, when the next meeting came around, he'd tell her that he'd go alone so that she wouldn't realize that he had no intention of attending.

"Hi, Dio, nice to see you again," a voice behind him pulled him out of his reverie. He turned on his heels and looked at the young woman who greeted him.

"Hi." He couldn't put a name to the pretty face, nor could he recall whether they had indeed met.

"Lisa," she prompted. "You probably don't remember my name…"

"I'm sorry, but—"

"Lisa, uh, can you help us here?" Ariadne asked, pointing to the delivery man who stood at the entrance to a door leading into the back, a storage area most likely.

"Excuse me," Lisa said and joined her boss.

Wanting to feel useful, Dio decided to interrupt them before they got too deep into their work. "Ariadne, shall I get us all some takeout food? Looks like neither of you will have time for a sit down lunch anyway." He pointed at the cases of wine, some partially opened, some still closed, that littered the entrance to the storage room.

"That would be wonderful. Thanks." Ariadne smiled at him before looking back over the paperwork in her hands.

He found himself smiling back at her, drinking in her sweet features. After lunch, he'd make a play for dessert.

By the time Dio returned from a little Italian

restaurant, several pasta dishes and salads in hand, the delivery man had left, and Lisa and Ariadne were carrying the heavy cases into the storage room. He dropped the food onto the counter and rushed toward them.

"Let me do that," he offered and took the case right out of Ariadne's arms. "Why don't the two of you start with lunch and I'll join you once I've put the wine away?"

"You brought lunch for me too?" Lisa asked, surprise evident in her raised voice.

"Of course. We need to put some meat on your bones." He winked. The girl was entirely too skinny for his taste. Now, Ariadne's lush curves, they were a totally different thing. When his gaze traveled up Ari's hips and breasts and landed on her face, he noticed her miffed expression. Had he said something wrong? She couldn't possibly have taken his comment to Lisa the wrong way, could she? Or was he prone to flirt with other women? "Now, both of you, eat."

He walked into the store room when Ariadne called after him, "But you don't know where to put them."

"Sorted by country, then by varietal, then by year?" It was how his own wine cellar was stocked. *His own wine cellar?* Where would he have a wine cellar? There was no space in his small apartment in Charleston to have such a luxury. All he had was a wine fridge. Yet he knew with one hundred percent certainty that he had a wine cellar. Somewhere.

"Yes, just like that," Ariadne confirmed.

The smell of the food wafted into the storeroom as he hefted case after case into it and stacked them up high. Soon, his stomach growled, and he was glad when the last case was in its place.

He emerged from the storage room and stopped for a moment to watch Ariadne and Lisa enjoy their lunch at the tasting counter. While Lisa was a pretty girl, and very young at that, his eyes were drawn to Ariadne and her figure. Everything about her was more mature and riper than the fresh girl by her side. Ripe for the plucking. And what a plentiful harvest it would be.

His groin tightened at the thought. If he didn't get his hands on her soon, he'd burst into flames.

"Have you left me anything?" He walked over to them and peered into the cartons.

"You brought way too much," Ariadne claimed.

"I'm famished." For more than just food. Dio forced himself to shovel some pasta onto a paper plate and dig into it. The sooner he'd eaten his main course, the sooner he'd be able to move onto dessert. Which wouldn't stop him from looking at his dessert while eating his entrée.

Lisa cleaned off the last of the pasta from her plate when the little bell over the door tinkled, announcing the arrival of a customer. "I'll get that."

"I'll help you clean up," Dio offered Ariadne in the next instance.

"I've got it." Ari reached for an empty carton just as he did, their hands touching. She gave a nervous giggle before she tossed the carton into the trash behind her. The remaining containers and paper plates followed suit. "Done."

"Do you want to check on whether I put the cases in the right place?" Dio asked, a plan already forming in his mind.

"Yes, let me make sure I can find them later."

He followed her into the storeroom and quietly closed the door behind them. He didn't need an audience. As she walked between the aisles toward the far wall of the room, Dio admired the seductive sway of Ari's hips and the elegant curve of her legs. He knew exactly what he wanted her to do with those long legs. They looked strong and well toned, and he could fairly feel them wrapping around his hips as he thrust into her.

Despite the coolness in the room, a thin layer of perspiration built on Dio's forehead and neck. His heart raced and pumped blood to his cock in anticipation of what his brain was planning.

Ariadne stopped in front of the cases and perused them. Dio approached from behind and placed one hand to the side of her shoulder, touching the box behind her. "Did I do all right?" He purposefully lowered his voice, allowing it to sound more seductive than he'd ever spoken to her.

"Y-yes. It's fine." Her voice stuttered slightly, attesting to the fact that she was aware of his nearness and maybe even his intention.

"Tell me, baby, have we ever kissed in here?" He placed his hand on her shoulder and turned her to face him.

"N-no." Her eyes were downcast as if she couldn't meet his gaze, too afraid of what she'd see: the lust that was boiling over.

He shelved her chin on his palm and tilted her face up. "Why not?"

"We… we… I don't know." Her eyes skidded past him as if searching for an escape. There would be none.

"We'll have to remedy that." Without haste, he

dropped his head to hers. "We do kiss, don't we?"

"Y-yes."

He felt a surge of power at her answer. "Good. Because I have the feeling that I like kissing you. And I'm a little starved for a kiss right now." Then he crossed the remaining distance between them and brushed his lips to hers in a feather-light touch.

Her breath hitched at the contact, confirming that she was physically attracted to him. He would use this knowledge to free her from the stupid notion of practicing abstinence. In a few minutes, he'd have her panting for release.

Dio slid his hand to the back of her neck and slanted his head, sliding his lips over hers once more. His thigh brushed against her hip, the contact sending a flame of white heat through his groin. Of its own volition, his other thigh nudged between her legs to press against her center.

A sigh escaped her mouth and bounced against his lips. He parted his lips to drink in her scent before pulling her upper lip into his mouth. Slowly, he slid his tongue over the soft flesh and felt her tremble in response.

"Easy, baby," he cooed and repeated his action.

When Ariadne parted her lips a moment later to take in a breath, Dio pressed his lips against her and allowed his tongue to glide into her. First slowly and with measured strokes, he explored her sweet cavern, tasting, touching, and caressing. An involuntary groan burst from his chest. By the gods, he enjoyed kissing her even more than he thought was humanly possible. As he pressed her against the cases at her back, he intensified his kiss and let all ideas of a slow seduction fly into the wind.

Instead, he captured her, allowing her no reprieve, and issued his demand. With determined strokes, he slid against her tongue, initiating a passionate dance, one she answered without hesitation. This wasn't the kiss of a woman who didn't know carnal pleasures. The kiss she shared with him was passionate and all-consuming, and the sounds coming from her body, the soft moans and sighs issuing from her chest, were not those of a shy virgin.

Dio ground his hips into her, letting one hand travel down her torso. As he caressed the outside of her breast with his thumb, Ariadne's arms went around his neck, one hand burying itself in his hair. He relished the feeling of her fingers digging into his scalp to hold him closer to her.

Encouraged by her reaction, he moved his hand over her breast, feeling the outline of her bra. The heat under his palm burned into his skin, but he needed more. Before she had a chance to stop him, had she intended to, he pulled her blouse out of the waistband of her skirt and tunneled underneath it. His fingertips met naked skin, soft and warm.

He moved his hand upwards, connecting with the underwire of her bra before he slid over the gauzy fabric and found the hard peak that had formed there. When his fingers brushed over it, a strangled moan issued from her lips together with a protest. "Stop."

But the word was so soft and accompanied by a thrust of her hips against his that he couldn't take the demand seriously. He could already smell her arousal, the sweet scent drifting into his nostrils, turning his entire body into a single-minded machine wanting only one thing: release.

"Shh, baby," he whispered against her lips, briefly

interrupting the kiss. But a moment later, he was back, taking her lips more fiercely so she wouldn't be able to think of resistance.

His hand slid under the fabric of her bra and captured the ripe peak. Her flesh was firm and warm and more responsive than he'd dreamed. As he kneaded the globe that fit his hand perfectly, his cock turned into a rod so hard it could have been used as a crowbar. The charges of heat and energy racing through his body made his skin perspire and his heart beat in a frantic rhythm. His breathing was as labored as if he'd been running a Marathon, but he couldn't let that deter him from his goal. He had to have Ariadne, now, here. No matter what. Standing up, pressed against cases of wine, he'd fuck her until she admitted freely that abstinence had been a silly idea. And then he'd take her home and make love to her properly like a fiancé should.

Dio ripped his mouth from hers at the same time as he gripped the bottom of her blouse and pushed it upwards, exposing one breast. Then he pushed the bra aside, freeing one beautiful tit and dropping his lips to it. Capturing the hard nipple in his mouth, he sucked it.

Ariadne's head dropped against the cases as she let out a surprised gasp. But he wasn't about to give her a chance to pull back. As he sucked greedily and teased the nipple with his tongue, his hand went to her thigh. He found the seam of her swinging summer skirt and slid underneath it, moving his hand upwards toward the ultimate prize.

She wore no pantyhose, leaving her thighs bare to his touch. He caressed the soft skin and moved inwards, sliding his hand between her legs which she so obligingly parted wider. When his fingers connected with her panties, he realized that they were already soaked.

Her nipple popped out of his mouth. "Oh, baby!" Did she want him as much as he wanted her? Dio sucked her breast back into his mouth and slid one finger along the outside of her panties. The heat that greeted him was almost unbearable in its intensity. Once he buried his cock in her, he'd flare up like a single sheet of paper carelessly thrown into the fire, burning out just as quickly.

But not even that knowledge could make him slow down. He was past the moment of no-return, unable to control his urges any longer. Nothing could stop him from making Ariadne his now. Her response to him was unmistakable: she was aroused by his touch and wanted more. He wasn't going to deny her, and he for sure wasn't going to deny himself.

Dio pushed her panties lower and slid into them, passing the nest of curls until he felt the warmth and wetness that oozed from her core. His finger rubbed against her moist entrance, then pulled farther up to find her clit. He pressed against it with his dew-covered digit and heard her moan. In a few minutes, he'd breach her delicious portal and slide home.

"Ari, did you…" The voice in the background trailed off just as Ariadne jolted under his hold and stiffened.

"Sorry," Lisa added before the door was shut loudly.

Shit! The girl had terrible timing.

Ari pushed against him, making him release her. When he noticed her flushed face, she avoided his look and instead hastily adjusted her clothes. "I have to get back to work."

A second later, she brushed past him and left the room without a backwards glance.

7

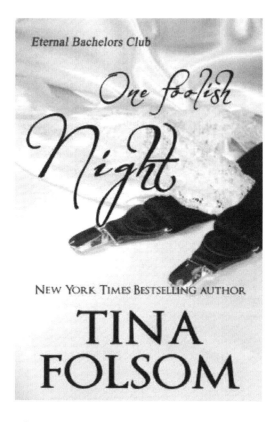

Eternal Bachelors Club

One foolish Night

NEW YORK TIMES BESTSELLING AUTHOR

TINA FOLSOM

He'd gone completely insane! There he was, standing in the foyer of his parents' house, ordering Holly to take his hard-on out of his pants and suck him.

Paul ran a shaky hand through his hair. Why was he behaving like a caveman with her? He was the suave seducer, the man who wined and dined his dates, who seduced them with tender touches and sweet words, with passionate kisses and expert lovemaking. He didn't order women to get on their knees to suck him—not because he didn't like a good blowjob (he did as much as the next guy), but because that particular pleasure wasn't something most women were willing to grant on a first date. Asking for it made any man look like a selfish lover. And he certainly wasn't that.

But there was something about Holly that turned him into a much more dominant and demanding lover than he liked to see himself. In fact, she drove him positively wild.

Holly's warm hands shoved his pants to midthigh, lowering his boxer briefs in the same movement. When her palms brushed the front of his thighs, he welcomed the electrical charge that raced through his body, and pressed himself more firmly against the oak door at his back.

He stared down at her, not wanting to miss a single second of their erotic encounter. His cock jerked when Holly dropped to her knees, bringing her head in line with his groin. Her mouth opened and her pink tongue appeared and swiped over the head of his cock in an almost leisurely action. The contact nearly made him choke on his next breath.

"Fuck!" He'd never felt anything as electrifying as the gentle caress of Holly's tongue. Instinctively, he pressed his hands flat against the wood, trying to stop himself from taking her head and shoving his cock into her mouth like the impatient man he was.

Instead, he took a steadying breath and watched as Holly licked all the way down the sensitive underside of his shaft, while her hands moved up his thighs until one brushed over his balls.

Paul nearly jumped out of his skin. He suppressed a curse and clenched his jaw. If he wasn't careful, this would be over sooner than he wanted it to be.

The vixen at his feet continued her tantalizing torture by licking his cock as if it were an ice cream cone, her warm tongue lubricating him, the texture of it making him hiss with pleasure. With every swipe she heightened his arousal, and with every second that passed, he grew more impatient to bury himself in her sweet heat.

He'd never wanted to fuck a woman as badly as he wanted to drive his cock into Holly, and he didn't care whether it was her mouth or her pussy he invaded first. Either seemed equally thrilling. Though he had to admit that seeing her kneel in front of him and feeling her tongue pleasure him made one option slightly more tempting at this moment than the other.

"Goddamn it, Holly! Don't play with me!" The words were out before he could stop himself. There was no way back now. If she thought him pushy, he couldn't help it, but he needed to be inside her. "Take me into your mouth or I'm going to rip your dress off and fuck you right here on the floor!"

His breath hitched when he suddenly felt her hand around the base of his shaft, gripping him firmly. Then her lips were around his cockhead, and a split second later he found himself engulfed in her hot, wet mouth.

A ragged breath tore from his chest, and his entire body visibly shuddered with pleasure. He had to brace himself more firmly against the door, afraid his knees would buckle, so intense were the sensations that rushed through him. His heart pounded in his chest, threatening to burst through his chest wall, and his pulse raced as if he were running the hundred-yard dash in under nine seconds. Sweat built on his neck and chest and started to soak his tuxedo shirt.

He felt more like an animal than a man when he reached for Holly and rested his hands on her shoulders. His hips started to move of their own volition, and he pumped into her mouth in a steady rhythm. Her breath caressed him in concert with her tongue, and the sucking motion of her lips teased his nerve endings, creating a tingling sensation that shot straight into his balls—balls Holly was still cradling and now started to squeeze with more pressure.

She knew exactly what a man liked. Somehow he'd known that the moment she propositioned him. When he'd looked at her lips, he'd realized instantly that those lips would suck him perfectly and give him the kind of pleasure only an experienced woman could give a man. Why some guys were fascinated with virgins, he couldn't fathom. He much preferred a woman who knew how to use her body for pleasure. Hers as well as his.

And to Holly's pleasure he would see shortly. Just as soon as he could command his cock to free itself from the enticing prison it found itself in.

Paul looked down at her, watching how her head rocked back and forth. Her blond curls brushed against his naked thighs with each movement, caressing him like a soft ocean breeze.

Her cheeks hollowed as she sucked him with more pressure, and the intensity of it made him press against her shoulders, pushing her back a few inches so his cock slipped out of her mouth.

"Fuck, Holly! Are you trying to kill me?" Because for certain, if she continued like this, his parents' staff would find him on the floor of the foyer in the morning, intense pleasure and lust having destroyed his body.

Holly glanced up at him, her lips glistening, her eyes glinting with the kind of wanton sheen only a seductress could conjure up. "Can't take any more? What a shame. I had a few more things planned for you."

Paul pulled her up and yanked her against him. "Maybe later. But right now, I need to get you onto your back with your legs spread wide and my cock deep inside you. Can we do that?"

"We can do anything we want," she murmured, and pressed her sex against his hard-on. "And by the looks of it, you'll be more than capable of doing all kinds of things with that big cock of yours."

That Holly found him big, he acknowledged with pride but without a word. Instead, he slid his hand into her hair and drew her head closer. "Don't you worry about that. Once you're in my bed, all you'll have to do is breathe. I'll take care of the rest."

She batted her lashes at him. "I hope that's not all macho-speak and is backed up by some action."

Paul brushed his lips over hers. "I'll give you all the action you can take."

Even if she'd wanted to respond to his last claim, he didn't give her the chance, because his mouth devoured hers a moment later, kissing her passionately and giving her a preview of what she could expect in his bed.

8

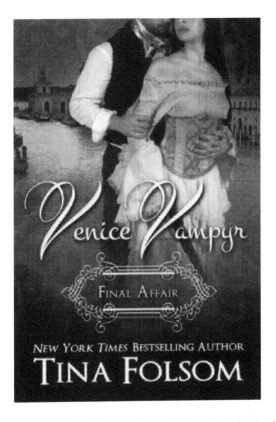

Dante waited for Viola, his long black cloak slung around his shoulders, the girl's cloak in his hands. He needed to get out of the house. If he stayed under the watchful eye of his brother and his sister-in-law any longer, he'd never get to kissing the girl and starting her education in the carnal arts.

It was time to remind her of what they'd done the night before—not when he'd penetrated her without much preparation, but when they'd kissed. If he wasn't mistaken, she'd liked the kissing part well enough.

He picked up her scent even before she exited the dining room. Just as her blood had tasted different when he'd licked it off her temple, her scent had something foreign to it. Something that made him want to protect her. He didn't understand his strange sentiment. After all, he was a self-proclaimed rake whose only interests lay in fornication and imbibing in rich blood until he felt the same kind of high drugs would produce in humans.

When he laid eyes on Viola as she resolutely swept into the foyer, his protective instinct toward her increased even more. The aura he sensed around her seemed fragile and in stark contrast to the sharp tongue she wielded against him so easily. Not that he minded. He'd spar with that tongue any day—or night.

Dante cleared his throat and pushed his thoughts back into the dark recesses of his debauched mind. "There you are."

"Where are we going?" Her voice was assessing.

He took a step toward her and secured the cloak around her shoulders, tying the ribbon under her throat. Then he dipped his head to whisper in her ear. "Exploring."

Before she could protest, he swept her outside into the night. Minutes earlier, he'd secured a gondola and a gondolier who'd promised him a smooth ride through the canals and a discrete look in the other direction when necessary.

Dante helped Viola into the gondola and squeezed onto the comfortable high-back bench next to her. She was a dainty thing, yet his massive proportions assured there wasn't an inch of space between them.

As the gondolier pushed off and navigated them down the canal, Dante made himself comfortable and slid his arm around Viola's shoulders to press her closer to him.

"Signore!" she protested.

He dipped his head to hers. "Please call me Dante. I'd hate for you to scream 'Signore' when you come apart in my arms. Now, enjoy the ride."

She didn't respond, and he didn't expect her to. For now, all he wanted was for her to enjoy the tour. Since she'd admitted that she was staying in a hotel, he knew she was not native to Venice. It had given him the idea of taking her on a little sightseeing tour along the picturesque canals. Even at night, she would be able to see many of the magnificent mansions and palaces the city was famous for.

As he pointed out different buildings and retold little anecdotes about the inhabitants, he felt her relax next to him. From the corner of his eye, he noticed how she looked at many of the impressive homes with awe, her mouth open in obvious admiration. Illuminated on the inside by massive chandeliers, Dante and Viola caught glimpses of the grandeur inside.

"Beautiful," she whispered.

Dante was pleased with himself. Viola seemed to enjoy the gondola ride. It was part of his plan to show her that life was worth living, that there was beauty and excitement all around her.

When she suddenly shivered next to him, he pulled her closer. "Cold?"

She nodded, and he reached for her folded hands. They were like ice. He cursed himself. Just because he didn't feel the cold as severely as a human would didn't mean he could forget about her well-being. "I'm sorry, Viola."

He opened his own cloak.

"No, you'll be cold then," she protested.

"No, I won't. Come." Before she could protest, he lifted her into his arms and settled her on his lap. He scooted back onto the bench before he closed his cloak over both of them.

"But—"

He killed her protest by pressing her closer to his chest, keeping his own arms inside his cloak, away from prying eyes. "This way we'll both be warm."

"Is that why?" She tilted her chin up in challenge.

"There's a second reason."

"Which would be?"

"Did you like it when I kissed you last night?"

She dropped her lids at his question but said nothing.

"Do you want me to kiss you again?"

An almost unperceivable nod was the answer. Excitement coursed through him. He hadn't misread her the night before. He had another chance. "Then lift your head and offer me your lips."

She did just that. But instead of stealing a passionate and demanding kiss, he pushed back his hunger for her and only lightly brushed his lips against hers. They were almost as frozen as her hands. He nibbled on them, stroking over them with his hot tongue in an attempt to warm her.

~ ~ ~

Viola closed her eyes and savored the gentle touch. Dante was different than the night before, less urgent, less demanding. Gentler, softer. Yet in no way less intoxicating. She breathed in his rich scent, a mixture of musky cologne—the same she'd smelled in his bed—and a deep earthy and leathery scent.

His lips were tentative against her, merely touching lightly, barely pressing against her. A frustrated moan escaped her. She wanted him to kiss her the way he'd kissed her the night before.

"Something wrong?" he whispered against her lips.

"No." She couldn't very well tell him what she wanted. Instead, her hands went to his shirt and pulled, forcing him to put more heat behind the kiss. Hadn't she just told him she was cold? Did he think his little timid kiss would get her warm?

When she pressed her lips against his mouth, a startled moan came from his throat. Suddenly, he angled his head and nudged at her lips, requesting entry with his tongue. On a relieved sigh, she parted her lips and welcomed him.

Her hand dug into his shirt to hold him close to her so he wouldn't stop too soon. In seconds, his kiss had turned from innocent to demanding. Instantly, she felt heat build in her belly and ripple through her body, reaching all her cells. She relaxed into him, melted against his mouth and tongue, opened up for him so he could explore her more thoroughly. All the while, her hands stroked him through his shirt. She marveled at the hardness of his muscled chest and the warmth his body radiated. She wanted to soak up all of it and cocoon herself in his warmth and closeness.

When his hand moved up the side of her torso and reached the underside of her breast, she gasped into his mouth. But he didn't stop. On the contrary, he increased the demand in his kiss, making her forget where she was.

His hand cupped her breast and gave it a soft squeeze. She yelped and pulled away from his mouth. "No, not here. People can see."

"Nobody can see what I'm doing under the cloak," he assured her, and took her mouth again, stifling her next protest. As if to underscore his statement, he tugged on the bodice and managed to free her breasts, letting the material bunch just under them. It now provided a shelf on which her breasts rested for him to do with as he pleased.

"Dante!" She tried to tell him that it wasn't decent but he kissed her again. With every kiss, she was less able to resist him. Her body seemed to melt more and more every second he exerted this sweet torture on her.

When his hand brushed over her breast and grazed her nipple, a bolt of lightning shot through her core. It liquidized everything in its path and left an unknown ache behind. Viola writhed under his touch, trying to soothe the want his touch left behind.

"Easy, my sweet," he cooed and nibbled kisses along her neck while his fingers teased her naked flesh, turning her nipple into a hard peak. "I'll give you what you want."

How could he know what she wanted when she didn't know it herself? All she knew was that she didn't want him to stop touching her. So when his hand left her breasts and lowered to her waist, she protested. "No. Please. I want—"

His hand squeezed her thigh, the warmth flooding through her making her forget her thoughts. "I know what you want."

Did he? She hoped so, because she was burning up. Her insides were aching, the place between her legs throbbing with desperate need. Her heart beat frantically, and her lungs burned as she panted.

A moment later, she held her breath. Dante's hand traveled down her leg and scooted under her skirts. Panic gripped her. "What are you doing?"

"Making you feel good." He nibbled on her ear, biting on it lightly. The sting distracted her from the movement of his hand, but only for a moment.

When his fingers suddenly reached the apex of her thighs and tunneled underneath her drawers, she gasped at his boldness. "Dante," she whispered, less in protest than encouragement, for his fingers had reached the dewy moisture that was oozing from her. She tensed when she felt him probe at her cleft, afraid of the penetration that had hurt the night before. She froze, steeling herself against the pain, but nothing happened. He'd stilled his fingers.

"Shh," Dante breathed into her ear. "I won't enter you. I just want to feel your wetness and caress you."

Slowly, Viola relaxed against his hand. Warring emotions filled her mind. She should push him away, not allow him such intimacy. Yet, the night before she'd allowed him much more than that. She had no strength to resist him, because just as she had the night before when he'd kissed her, she wanted more of what he was doing now.

And wasn't this what she'd come to Venice for? To experience the pleasures of the flesh? The loss of her virginity the night before had been unpleasant, but what Dante was doing with his fingers now felt more than pleasant. The caress of his fingers against her intimate flesh made her body heat further and her heart increase its frantic beat.

"You like that?" Dante's husky voice unleashed another heat wave in her body.

Before she could stop herself, she admitted, "Yes."

"I like it too. You're so slick, so soft. And then..." He drew his dew-covered finger further up, away from her folds to a spot just below her curls. "Then there's this." He rubbed against the sensitive flesh, making her gasp. "Yes, I think I've found just what you need."

As he swirled his finger around the bundle of flesh that was more sensitive than any other part of her body, it throbbed even harder than it had earlier. She felt more moisture oozing from her core. Her head fell back against his shoulder, and she let out a ragged breath.

"So responsive," he praised and continued his sweet torture. She felt boneless in his arms. Her thighs spread wider to allow him better access to this special place. His growl told her that he approved of her action.

As if to thank her for it, his caress became more urgent, the pressure harder. Something was happening. Her body tensed, both in fear and in anticipation. She didn't know what to expect. Viola only knew one thing. "Don't stop!" she cried out.

Seconds later, her body erupted. The tension splintered into waves of unknown pleasure and delight, flowing through her in ripple after ripple.

Behind her eyes, she saw an explosion of white light so intense she thought she would die. This was her end.

9

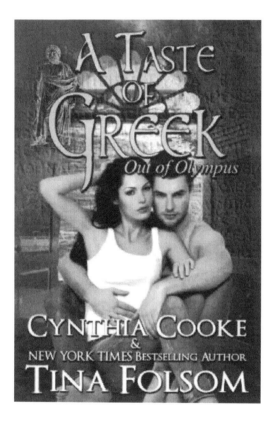

Penny stood in front of him, purse in hand, a look of wide-eyed shock on her face. "Hermes!" Her voice shook as she said his name.

"Where are they?" he growled, barely able to keep himself from lunging at her, grabbing her shoulders and shaking the truth out of her.

He was livid! On top of it, he'd been caught in the torrential downpour Zeus had created and hadn't had a chance to dry himself with his godly powers, because several students had meandered in the hallway on his way to Penny's office.

"What?" she said, backing away from him.

She was afraid. He could clearly see it in her face, the way her eyes searched for an escape route, and the way her lips trembled slightly. Hell, he could practically smell the fear coming off of her in waves.

"As if you didn't know," he said, gritting his teeth, barely able to contain his fury.

"I don't know. Really." She was up against the wall now. Her gaze moved from his face to the door behind him. As if she could escape. As if he would let her go!

He took a step toward her.

"Hermes," she started, holding her purse in front of her. All breathless, her lips puckered, her chest heaved. "You're drenched. Can I get you a towel?" She set her purse down on the desk and tried to hurry past him.

One hand shot out and grabbed her by the shoulder, stopping her as she passed. "No. I don't want a towel." He leaned forward, his face inches from hers, water dripping from his hair onto her shoulder. "You know what I want."

"Please, Hermes," she said, turning to look up at him. "I know I shouldn't have left you this morning the way I did. I just," she hesitated. "There was just something important I'd completely forgotten. Time sensitive work. And then I was coming right back. In fact, I was hoping to get back before you even woke—"

"Stop!" he bellowed.

"What?" she squeaked.

Terrified eyes looked at him. Her breath quickened, and he noticed the vein on the side of her neck pulsing violently. For a brief second, he felt like an ass. He didn't scare women. He loved women. Not once in his entire life had he ever hurt a woman.

Not once had he wanted to.

"Did you plan on doing it all along?" he asked, pushing the words through his clenched jaw.

She didn't answer him, just looked at him all doe-eyed and confused. How good an actress was she? How long would she keep up the pretense and put on this show of innocence?

"Did you sleep with me just so you could take them? Did you want to be with me at all?" He hated the pleading sound in his voice.

Almost as much as he hated the sudden understanding and pity that swept into her eyes. As if she knew that he was head over heels for her, and didn't want what he was offering, but had to find a way of letting him down easy.

"No," she whispered, her head moving from side to side. "Never. I adore you Hermes. You are amazing." She raised a trembling hand to his cheek. Was she afraid that he would slap it back?

Damn it, he couldn't let her think that!

In one swift movement, he pushed her against the wall, his face mere inches from hers. She gasped an astonished breath, and then his lips fell over hers. Devouring her. Punishing her. Showing her who he really was. Not a man to be trifled with. But a god. A god!

Penny moaned, her lips parting, allowing his

tongue to thrust into her mouth, sparring with her. He lost himself in her. His hand roamed her body, touching her breasts, kneading them harshly. She moaned, pushing herself closer, begging for more.

Her hands undid the buttons of his shirt, pulling the wet fabric off his shoulder. She stroked his chest, her fingers playing with his nipples, making him momentarily forget everything.

Hermes ripped his mouth from hers. "Damn it, Penny! Where are my sandals?"

"I don't have them."

He didn't believe her, but by the gods, he'd get the truth out of her, one way or another. All was fair in love and war. Whether this was love or war, he wasn't entirely sure. But it didn't matter right now, because the result was the same: he'd fuck the truth out of her if he had to.

Reaching for the seam of her dress, he pulled the garment up over her thighs. His hand slipped between her legs, stroking over her panties—panties that were drenched already. God damn it, was this turning her on like it turned him on?

With one yank, he ripped the flimsy piece of lingerie from her body, tossing it to the floor.

"Tell me the truth!" he demanded again.

"I didn't take them," she insisted.

Angry at her refusal, he lifted her up and laid her over the desk, pushing papers off it to make space.

"You have one more chance," he warned, and stepped between her legs. His fingers already opened the top button of his jeans and lowered the zipper.

Without taking his eyes off her, he shoved his pants and boxer briefs to mid-thigh, freeing his erection. By the gods, he was hard! He pulled a condom from his pocket, ripped the foil package open, and sheathed himself.

"Tell me the truth! Where are they?"

"I don't have them. Maybe another partygoer took them."

Her chest heaved, her puckered nipples—evidence of her arousal—pushing through the fabric of her dress. He grabbed hold of her hips and plunged inside her, a scream dislodging from her lips at the same time.

"Oh God," she cried out, her eyelids fluttering. Her legs wrapped around him, her fingers digging into his ass, trying to pull him in closer, pushing herself up to meet each and every thrust he delivered.

"Damn it, Penny!"

Suddenly this didn't feel like the punishment he'd intended to dole out. The aroused look in her eyes and the plentiful juices in her warm pussy were evidence enough that she was enjoying this. He couldn't allow this! She wasn't meant to enjoy this. She was meant to feel his wrath!

He plowed into her, harder, deeper, faster. But her expression didn't change. She didn't push him away, didn't try to get away from him. Instead she moaned, pulling her lower lip between her teeth as if trying to prevent herself from screaming out her pleasure.

His balls tightened at the erotic image before him. Fuck! He was going to come again. He should deny her, hold back, not give her what she wanted. But his body had other ideas. His hips delivered thrust after thrust, his cock only thinking of its own pleasure.

"Who told you to steal them?"

Her lips parted. "Nobody."

He let himself go, let his body take over, allowing his control to slip through his fingers. Seconds later, he felt his seed shoot through his cock and fill her, just as he'd done the night before.

He looked down at her. Her cheeks were flamed, her hair mussed, her legs still wrapped around him. And her pussy still quivered with aftershocks of her own orgasm. He'd fucked her like he was some randy dog.

The ring of a cell phone interrupted his thoughts.

Penny's eyes widened in panic. "That's Grams." She reached for her bag, trying to lift herself to a sitting position.

"We're not done talking," he growled, pulling out of her. In fact, they hadn't even started to talk, since his body had had other ideas. Stupid ideas!

"I have to take this call. The ringtone, it's my grandmother. Something must be wrong."

Reluctantly, Hermes stepped back and allowed her to reach for her phone, while she tried to push down her dress at the same time, covering her nakedness.

10

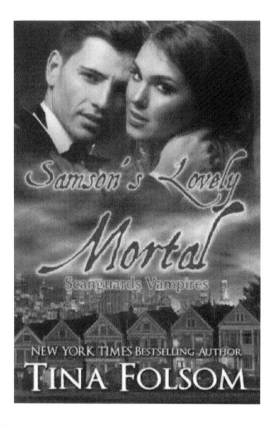

He stepped out of the bathroom and broke into a huge smile when he saw his visitor.

"Delilah."

With a few strides he crossed the room and took her into his arms. His mouth was less than an inch away from her tempting lips. "How was your day?"

"Don't ask." She sounded exhausted. He knew just the right remedy for that.

Samson brushed a feather light kiss on her lips. "I missed you." He had, despite the fact that he'd been up only a few minutes.

"Hmm, that's better," Delilah murmured as he sought her lips again. Her hands embraced him and slowly moved from his back farther south. He felt her slip them into his boxers, touching his firm ass. Ah, but her hands were soft.

"You're not dressed."

"You noticed that, huh?" He chuckled. "I was just about to take a shower." But why shower alone when she was back? "Care to join me?"

Should he just lug her over his shoulder, or would he be acting too much like a caveman? Woman. Sex. It was all he could think of.

Samson didn't wait for an answer, but started to pull down the zipper of her skirt and let it drop to the floor. Her blouse followed seconds later. She didn't show any objection.

"I guess I must have said yes." She smiled as she stepped out of her shoes.

"That's what I heard."

When he stripped her of her bra and panties, Delilah returned the favor and let his boxers drop to the floor. His hard-on jutted out proudly and pointed straight at her. Samson lifted her up and carried her into the bathroom.

He put her back on her feet before he turned on the water in the shower, but kept his arm around her waist. Her skin was too tempting to let go of.

"I had a hard time this morning doing my hair in here. I couldn't find a mirror."

Samson flinched. Damn, she'd noticed. Since vampires didn't reflect in mirrors, he'd never had a need to have one installed in his bathroom. What else had she noticed?

"Sorry about that. I'm having it replaced. I wasn't planning on an overnight guest."

He smiled at her and kissed her quickly before she could find anything else that struck her as odd. His kiss silenced her just the way it was intended to. He pulled her into the shower without releasing her lips.

His hunger for her had just doubled. Had it only been last night that he'd first had sex with her? It seemed that he knew her body much more intimately than that. Every curve was familiar, yet so exciting. He knew he would recognize her touch even if he were blind. The way her hands teased his skin, how her fingers ignited his passion for her—he would always know it was she.

"Why don't you help me get cleaned up?"

Without waiting for an answer, Samson squeezed a dollop of liquid soap into her hand. As her hands lathered the soap over his skin, he closed his eyes. Never had he felt so relaxed than when he was with her. He breathed in deeply when he felt her hands tending to his shaft and balls. Delilah slowly and deliberately moved her hand up and down, the foam making the movement smooth.

"Good?"

His little human vixen was clearly bent on driving him insane and doing an excellent job at it.

"You have no idea." He sighed and allowed himself to be swept away by her touch. His hands sought her out and pressed her against him.

"Rinse me off. I don't want to be full of soap

when I slide inside you."

It felt completely natural that he wanted her and let her know what he intended to do. There was no pretense between them.

He saw Delilah smile as she rinsed the soap off his skin. She could get him excited within seconds. Samson lowered his head to her mouth, smothering her with his passionate kiss.

His tongue mated with hers, filling her mouth, just like he wanted to fill the rest of her body. She tasted like a beautiful summer night, like rain after a hot day. Her scent alone drove him to distraction, but coupled with her sweet taste and the softness of her naked skin pressed against his, brought him right back to the night before. There was only one cure for his desire for her. He had to bury himself in her, and he couldn't wait a minute longer.

His cock throbbed almost painfully when he lowered himself a few inches and guided himself in between her thighs so her moist pink petals rested on him. Samson slid back and forth, staying outside her body, letting her ride his hard rod.

"You feel so good." She moaned.

Exactly his thought. No. Not *good. Amazing!* Her soft flesh was warm, her wetness drenching him.

He shifted his angle, and his shaft teased at the entrance of her body. Delilah breathed heavily.

"We should get a condom," she whispered, but her body pressed against his cock. Did she know what she was doing, or was she just as lost in the sensation as he was?

"We should." But instead he eased into her just an inch deep. He would go get a condom from the bedroom if she insisted. "I'll get one." But he didn't move, and her hands held onto his arms. Her muscles tensed around him, as if to pull him closer.

"Samson, don't leave." Her voice was hoarse, but insistent. She pushed toward him, making him penetrate deeper.

He was halfway inside her and felt her muscles tantalize him. Hell, he was on fire.

"You want me like this, right now?" Samson waited for her protest, but it didn't come. In slow motion he inched forward, easing himself deeper and deeper into her as he gazed into her eyes. So beautiful, so passionate, and all his.

"I want nothing more."

Her kiss was tender and loving as they rocked to the rhythm of their heartbeats. He pulled up her leg and wrapped it around his hip, thrusting deeper into her. His arms supported her weight. Delilah's lips brought him back into the field of lavender and made him feel the sun on his back, just like the night before. Samson was lost in the sensation as she carried him away.

Her nails dug into his ass as she held onto him, urging him deeper into her. Never had he been with a woman who'd shown such passion, and who he was willing to give everything in his power.

Delilah's moans were like a drug to him, her kisses like a most exquisite wine, and her body ultimate ecstasy. He would never need anything else, only her, like this, right now.

Too late, he heard the door to the bedroom open and the heavy steps come toward the bathroom.

"Samson, you're not gonna like this—" Ricky's voice penetrated his bliss.

In lightning speed, Samson spun around to shield

Delilah from Ricky's view.

"Get the fuck out, Richard!" he growled low and dark. Even in his own ears he sounded more like an animal than a man. Ricky knew all too well that whenever Samson called him by his full name, he meant business. He did well retreating instantly.

"I'm so sorry, sweetness," Samson whispered to Delilah, making sure his voice was soft again.

She was completely still in his arms, obviously shocked at the interruption. He couldn't blame her. "I'm going to have a serious word with him."

~ ~ ~

Delilah looked up at him, and his eyes were their usual hazel color again, but in the instant when he'd yelled at Ricky, she'd seen them flash red. Like an alarm. Like a stop light. It had shocked her more than Ricky barging in on them. Still thinking of his strange eyes, she went stiff in his arms. This wasn't normal. How could somebody's eye color change like that?

She was glad that Samson didn't look at her now, but again had his cheek pressed against hers, for she wasn't sure she could have hidden her alarmed expression.

"Give me a few minutes. I'll get rid of him. And then I'm all yours."

He kissed her cheek softly and pulled out of her.

"No problem." Suddenly she felt cold. And alone.

Delilah watched him reach for the towel and step out of the shower. She turned away and let the water engulf her, pretending to enjoy the shower. In reality she tried to calm her nerves. When she looked back a few seconds later, Samson had already left the bathroom. She braced herself against the tile wall.

Had she hallucinated? She'd clearly seen the fury

in his eyes, and considering the violation of their privacy, she could understand him lashing out at Ricky, but she couldn't understand the red in his eyes. Had he popped a blood vessel? No, impossible. Seconds later, his normal hazel color had returned, and all the red was gone.

She pressed her hand against her sex where she could still feel his pistoning cock. Something wasn't right. Something about Samson was different, and it suddenly scared her.

11

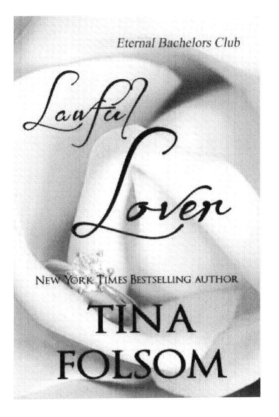

Eternal Bachelors Club

Lawful Lover

NEW YORK TIMES BESTSELLING AUTHOR

TINA FOLSOM

Shifting in her seat, she looked at him. "Seriously though, Daniel, what are we going to tell your parents when they ask us how we met?"

"We'll tell them the truth," he said calmly.

When she looked back at him in horror, he laughed. "That my friend Tim set us up on a blind date."

She gave him a scolding slap on his shoulder. "I thought our relationship is nothing to joke about."

He snatched her hand and kissed it, a twinkle in his eyes. "See, I do have a sense of humor. Of course we'll leave out the fact that Tim lied to me about what he was doing and that I didn't know I was being set up."

"And the fact that I was pretending to be an escort," she added.

There was no way she could ever tell anyone about this part of their history, especially not his parents. It was bad enough that she'd agreed to it in the first place, and she thanked her lucky stars that Daniel had still wanted her despite the fact that she'd pretended to be an escort. Most other men would have never considered her girlfriend material after that, let alone asked her to live with him.

"It will remain our secret." He reached out and caressed her cheek with the back of his hand. "Please relax, baby. My parents are going to love you as much as I do."

"You really think so?"

"I know so." Daniel speared his fingers into her hair and brought her closer to him. He slanted his lips over hers and parted them with his tongue, expertly exploring her mouth as if he'd spent his entire life kissing her and only her.

Sparks ignited deep within her core, and she cursed the fact that they weren't alone. She wanted nothing more than to rip the clothes from his body and have him make love to her. She wanted Daniel to whisper sweet words to her as he pleasured her and drove her to ecstasy. Just as he'd done during the last two weeks.

She ran her hand down his chest and stomach and grazed his crotch. She felt his cock jerk at her touch. Daniel groaned. She had to restrain herself from sliding her hand over him once more or she was going to end up giving their fellow passengers a show they would never forget.

"You're killing me," he whispered, giving her a look that made his desire for her crystal clear.

"You started it," she reminded him.

"Yeah, and I plan to finish it, too." Daniel stood and held out his hand to her. "Come."

"What? Why? Where are we going?" she asked under her breath, darting frantic looks around her.

They were on a plane thousands of feet in the air. Where could he possibly take her? Sabrina stood and reluctantly followed him along the aisle, trying to look inconspicuous, when realization hit her.

"You can't be serious," she whispered.

"Oh, I'm very serious." Daniel looked around furtively to make sure they weren't being watched.

Then he ushered Sabrina into the tiny restroom at the front of the first class cabin, squeezed in behind her, and locked the door behind them. He pinned her against the door.

"You undo me, Sabrina." He dragged his mouth across her jaw and down her neck. "I have no control when it comes to you."

Sabrina moaned and reached for his shirt, fumbling with it until it was open. God, he had a muscular chest, not too beefy, but just ripped enough to make any woman weak in the knees. She appreciatively ran her hands across his chest and down his stomach until she reached the top of his pants. Tilting her head to give him better access, she undid his pants and freed his cock. He was fully erect. Sabrina wrapped her fingers around his hard-on and gave it a firm stroke, up, then down, then back up again, her palm working over the velvety-smooth head.

Daniel put both of his hands flat on the door above her head and looked down, watching as she caressed him. He sucked in a breath.

"That feels good," he said, claiming her lips again. He left her mouth and kissed a path down her throat, stopping only once he reached the neckline of her sundress.

She arched her back, awash in sensations. "Yes," she hissed.

Daniel continued down her body, dropping to sit on the toilet behind him. He looked up at her through thick lashes with a sexy half smile on his face as he pulled her closer, lifted her left leg and draped it over his shoulder.

Sabrina sucked in a breath and held it as Daniel lifted her dress.

"How about we get rid of these panties?"

The last time he'd made that suggestion, she hadn't gotten them back. He had quite the collection by now.

Sabrina chuckled softly. "Am I going to get this pair back?"

"Probably not."

He pulled them down and off her legs then shoved them into his pocket. Daniel lowered his head to her sex. His fingers parted her wet folds, before he licked over her clit then drove one finger into her. Bright flashes of white light appeared before her eyes as her hands and nails fought to grasp for support. She clutched the sink with one hand and pressed against the wall with the other.

"Oh God, oh God, oh God!" she chanted, trying to hold back the scream that was building in her.

"Shhhhh." His breath whispered over her sensitive sex, sending an uncontrollable shiver through her body.

She loved it when Daniel licked her. He always knew exactly what she needed and how she needed it. She'd never been with a man as attuned to her body as Daniel.

Her hips moved in a steady rhythm, urging him to finger-fuck her and lick her harder, faster, deeper. She couldn't get enough.

"You taste so good," he said, his words vibrating against her folds.

It was too much. Though she wanted to hold on, to suspend the pleasure, she couldn't. Her orgasm broke hard and fast. Her legs shook from the intensity.

"Yeah, that's it, baby. Come for me, Sabrina."

She shoved her hands into his hair and bit on her lip to stop herself from screaming his name as she rode out the waves of her orgasm.

Daniel gently put her foot back on the floor, while she fought to catch her breath. He stood, pulled her leg to his thigh, and plunged his cock into her with one thrust before she'd even had a moment to register what he was planning. Sabrina grabbed his shoulders and dug her nails into his flesh. The wall moaned against her back.

"Wrap your legs around me," he said, and she complied. Then he turned them around and sat her on the edge of the minuscule sink.

Daniel found her lips again and kissed her in the same rhythm as his cock plunged in and out of her.

"God, I love being inside you," he said, steadily increasing the tempo and intensity of his thrusts.

She wanted to scream her approval, but knew she couldn't.

They were having sex in an airplane bathroom!

She'd never done anything so crazy before. Well, maybe except for that one time when they'd trespassed and she and Daniel had had sex out in the open, looking out over the San Francisco Bay and Alcatraz. Daniel had a way of making her throw all her inhibitions to the wind.

When she felt him groan and drive into her one last time, a warm spray of his semen accompanying his final thrust, her sex convulsed around his cock, joining him in his release.

Daniel dropped his forehead to hers, breathing heavily. "Are you okay?"

"Yeah." She nodded. "Kiss me."

His lips found hers again and he moved inside her in slow and almost lazy strokes. "God, Sabrina, I can't get enough of you. I could stay here like this, buried inside you forever."

"Daniel," she murmured. "This is crazy."

"I know." Slowly, he pulled out of her and met her gaze. "You're so beautiful, you know that?"

"Thank you." She felt herself flush at his compliment. No matter how many times he told her that he found her beautiful, it always felt like the first time.

Daniel cleaned himself off and helped her do the same, then reached for his pants, pulling them up, and re-buttoning them.

Sabrina hopped off the sink and readjusted her dress. Then she held out her hand. "My panties please."

He gave her a wicked grin as he pulled them from his pocket and put them in her hand. "I'm going to take those back as soon as we get home."

His words dripped with promise—a promise that she intended to hold him to. She slipped her panties back on when a thought struck her. "Daniel? When we leave this bathroom… people are going to know what we were doing, aren't they?"

Daniel wrapped his arms around her. "So? Personally, I want people to know you're mine."

How could she argue with that? Still, even though she'd just joined the mile-high-club, she didn't want to announce it to everybody. "Daniel…"

He chuckled, but his eyes shone with understanding. "Okay, if it makes you feel better, you can go out first and I'll come out a few minutes after you."

"Thank you."

She opened the door a sliver and peered outside.

12

Oliver slanted his lips over hers and took her mouth in a kiss, first gently and softly in case she changed her mind, but when she didn't, he pulled her closer and deepened the kiss.

He couldn't believe this turn of events. From the moment Ursula had entered the abandoned building, he'd instinctively known that she was telling the truth. He'd sensed her fear. Finding the wallet from a client of the blood brothel—as he would call it—was confirmation enough for him that he could trust her.

But finding out that she hadn't been raped, that none of those despicable vampires had laid their dirty paws on her, made him rejoice. At the same time he cursed them for denying her any sort of carnal pleasure.

He severed the kiss and looked at her. "Let's go home." Then he would take her to his bed and make sure she got the release she needed.

To his surprise Ursula shook her head. "I can't wait. Please." She eyed the bench in the back of the van.

Oliver's heart skipped a beat. "Now? Here? In the van?"

More blood pumped into his cock, making him harder than a crow bar. At the same time hunger surged through him. He had to feed, and soon, or he wouldn't be master of his own actions anymore.

"Yes," she murmured and slid her hand onto his thigh, then moved it upwards.

When her fingers reached the outline of his hard-on, he groaned, his hunger instantly forgotten. "Get in the back."

He locked the doors, then followed her. When he saw her hand opening the top button of her jeans, he stopped her. She stared at him in surprise.

"If you think I'm going to rush this, you're wrong."

"But—"

He smiled. "No *but*. If you want to sleep with me, then we're going through all the motions: the kissing, the touching, the seduction. I'm not going to pass up an opportunity to make love to the most beautiful girl I've ever seen and just fuck her like an animal."

Her expression softened, and her cheeks colored in a pretty pink, while her eyelids fluttered. "You want to make love to me?"

Oliver moved closer and shelved her chin on his palm. "And I want to make you come so hard that you think the world is exploding around you. Isn't that what you want?"

Her lashes swung up, almost touching her eyebrows. Her eyes shimmered. "Oliver?"

"Hmm?"

"Why are you so good to me?"

"Because you need somebody who's good to you." And more than anything, he wanted to be that person.

"Are we gonna talk all night, or are you going to kiss me?"

He chuckled. Ah, how he loved an eager woman! "In my mind I've never stopped kissing you."

She moved closer, her mouth less than an inch from his now. "Make it a reality then."

When he took her mouth again, the world around him blended into the background. Soft lips pressed against him, her hands pulled him closer, urging him to drag her body against his. With one movement, he pulled her onto his lap, so she straddled him. His hand on her lower back, he pressed her to him.

"That's better," he murmured.

Oliver captured her lips again and delved into the warm caverns of her mouth. He stroked and licked, tasted and explored. Her response was just as eager: with strong strokes, she played with his tongue. Lust surged through him, sending hot bolts of fire through his core and into the tip of his cock.

He moaned into her mouth, an action she echoed a few seconds later. Slanting his head, he sought a deeper connection, a fiercer kiss. Her hands dug into his shoulders as if she was holding on for dear life, and her response to him became even more passionate.

Then he suddenly felt her lick along his teeth. Shock catapulted through him when he felt a corresponding itching in his gums. He knew what this meant: his fangs were about to descend.

Ursula licked again. He severed the kiss, holding her a few inches away from him, breathing hard.

"Don't!"

Startled, she stared at him, apprehension spreading over her face. "What's wrong?"

He dropped his lids. God, how could he explain this to her without reminding her of what he was and what she was potentially unleashing in him?

"Please, am I doing something wrong?" Her voice cracked.

No, he couldn't disappoint her, couldn't let her cry again. But he had to be honest with her. When he raised his eyes to meet hers, he swallowed hard.

"When you lick my teeth like that, I can feel my fangs descend."

Her breath hitched.

"Fangs are the most erogenous zones in a vampire. They want to feel you licking them. But I can't allow that, because if I do…" He hesitated, searching her face for signs of fear.

"What'll happen?"

Oliver's gaze dropped to the pulsing vein at her

neck. "Once my fangs are out, it won't take long until I can't hold back my hunger for blood. I would bite you."

She sucked in a quick gulp of air.

Seeing that she was withdrawing from him, he quickly added, "But I won't. I promise you. I won't do that to you. You've been through enough. Please give me a chance. If we're careful…"

He hoped he wasn't lying. Could he truly hold back his hunger for the next hour so he could make love to her without subjecting her to the one thing she hated most: being bitten by a vampire?

"Careful, how?" she asked and approached slowly, her head dipping to the crook between his neck and shoulder. "Like this?" She pressed a gentle kiss on his skin, then another one.

Oliver closed his eyes, allowing the tender caress to sweep him away. "Perfect."

Her hands tugged on his T-shirt, pulling it from his jeans.

"Take it off," she whispered into his ear.

He did as she demanded, welcoming the cool air that touched his heated skin. But the relief didn't last, because a second later, her hands were on his chest, caressing him. His head fell back against the headrest. Wasn't he supposed to be the one seducing her, not the other way around? Clearly, things weren't going exactly as planned, not that he was complaining.

However, he'd made her a promise: to give her sexual pleasure. And he would not break his promise. It was time to take back the reins.

Oliver reached for her T-shirt, pulling it from her jeans. "Lift your arms."

She didn't hesitate and let him strip her of her T-shirt, exposing her bare breasts to him.

"Beautiful."

Her breasts were small, but perfectly formed, round and firm. He cupped one and squeezed lightly, then dipped his head to suck her nipple into his mouth. The little rosebud was already hard when he swiped his tongue over it. Her skin tasted of citrus fruits, pure and young. Innocent. The thought suddenly threw up a question.

"Are you a virgin?"

She shook her head. "No."

"Good," he murmured against her soft skin. "Because I would hate for you to feel pain when I'm inside you." No matter how short-lived that pain would be.

He returned to teasing her nipple, then paid her other breast the same attention, all the while listening and watching for her reactions so he could figure out what she liked most. He worked his way down to her stomach then shifted her with one move, placing her with her back down on the bench, so he could bend over her.

While his lips were blazing a trail down to her navel, his hands were already opening her jeans and lowering the zipper. When he pulled on her pants and looked up, he noticed her watching him, her lips parted, her breaths uneven. Desire shone from her eyes, and her cheeks were as flushed as her entire torso.

"I haven't done this in so long," she said, her voice low and almost apologetic.

He chuckled softly. "It's like riding a bike." Only tonight she would ride him. The thought sent another wave of heat through his body, igniting him even further.

He freed her of her jeans and panties, pulling off her shoes in the process, then let the items fall to the floor. She lay in front of him in the nude. He was glad for his vampire vision which allowed him so see her in her full glory despite the dim light.

Stroking his hands up from her calves to her thighs, he spread her legs apart then lowered his head toward the apex of her thighs.

"You're going to—?" She stopped herself.

Oliver lifted his eyes to look at her face. "You didn't think I would pass this up?" Not a chance. "When I said, we're going through all the motions, I meant it. And that includes tasting your sweet pussy."

The moment his mouth connected with her nether lips, Ursula moaned. Oliver licked at the dew that was already covering her plump flesh and let the taste spread over his tongue. His body hardened. Fuck! She tasted amazing. Spreading her as wide as was possible in the confined space they were in, he licked over her wet folds, nibbled, and explored. And with every soft moan and sigh that came from Ursula, his determination to make her climax rose.

He'd always loved sucking a woman, but the beautiful Asian girl in his arms was even more of a treat. To know that he could give her something she'd longed for for three years spurred him on. Licking higher up, he headed for her clit. The small bundle of nerves was already swollen, a sign of her arousal. He gently caressed it with his tongue. Ursula almost lifted off the bench, her body tensing.

"Easy, baby," he appeased her. "I'll be gentle."

Yet that gentleness cost him: inside him, the beast wanted to be unleashed and exert its prowess on her.

Holding back his wild side was a struggle he knew he would eventually lose. Still, he was determined to put up a fight. Because satisfying Ursula was more important right now than anything else. It would cement her trust in him; he was sure of it. And he wanted her to trust him.

With renewed determination, he continued to stroke his tongue over her tender organ, slowly putting more and more pressure on it. Ursula's breathing changed, becoming more uneven. Her heartbeat pulsed through her body in a rapid rhythm, the sound amplified by his vampire hearing. Her excitement fueled his own, and he was painfully aware of the hard-on that strained against the zipper of his jeans, which he was still wearing in order not to drive his aching cock into her before she had found her release. Once he was naked, there was no telling what he would do.

Like a cat, Ursula twisted underneath him, her moans getting louder, her sighs more pronounced. He doubled his efforts, realizing she was close.

"It's not working," she said. "I can't." Frustration and disappointment collided in her voice.

Fuck! He wasn't doing it right.

13

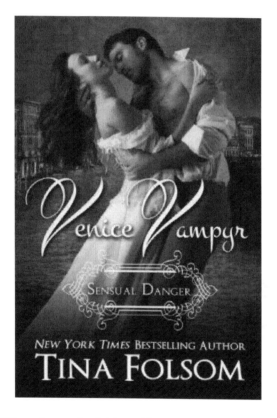

When he pushed himself away from the door and took a step into the room, Oriana's head suddenly whipped in his direction. Her eyes widened, but within a split second, she had herself under control again, hiding her outraged expression. She could have fooled any man and made him think she was indifferent to his presence, just not Nico, because at the same time he could hear her accelerated heartbeat as it beat a frantic tattoo against her ribcage. Her bosom heaved in concert with it.

"Good morning, Oriana," he greeted her and approached as slowly as a tiger its prey.

"Good morning, signore," she answered and turned to look at her plate, stabbing her fork into a morsel of biscuit, before she brought it to her lips and chewed longer than was necessary.

Clearly a ploy so she wouldn't have to converse with him. Little did she know that he hadn't come to talk.

"I trust you slept well," Nico continued and took a seat opposite her, reaching for a biscuit and putting it on his plate even though he had no intention of eating it.

He'd long ago mastered the art of moving food around his plate without anybody noticing that he never actually ate any of it. He distracted those who watched him with conversation and by cutting the food into smaller pieces, then rearranging it on his plate so that it looked as if he'd eaten some of it.

Not that he would even make a pretense of it today. He had, after all, more important things to do: he had to seduce his wife.

"Yes, very well. And you, did you sleep well?"

Her voice was a soft trickle, and he wondered how she would sound when she lay in his arms, panting in ecstasy. Would her voice be even more breathless? Even huskier? Or would she still pretend that he didn't affect her?

"I slept terribly, my sweet wife, and I hope to remedy this situation very soon."

When he lifted his lids and looked straight at her, he noticed a pink blush spread over her cheeks, but she didn't raise her eyes to meet his gaze and instead stared at her empty plate.

Then she removed the napkin from her lap and folded it, placing it neatly next to her plate. "If you'll excuse me. I have things to attend to."

She rose swiftly, but he was faster. Before she could make two steps away from the table, he had her cornered between it and the paneled wall.

"Signore! If you'd please let me pass," she requested, her voice tight.

"My name is Nico." He took another step closer, bringing his body flush with hers.

"Signore…"

He shook his head.

Finally she seemed to understand. "Nico, please, would you let me pass?"

"If that's what you truly want, Oriana." He closed the distance between their heads, allowing his lips to hover mere centimeters above her mouth. His action had caused her to press herself against the wall behind her, leaving her nowhere else to go.

"Y-yes," she stammered.

Nico leaned in closer. "How can you know what you truly want, my sweet, when you don't know what options you have? Why don't I show you some of them? Maybe then you can choose what you like best."

And he hoped her taste was similar to his.

His lips met hers, pressing softly against them. He wasn't going to behave like a barbarian and force himself on her. No, he'd rather tease her with his touch and coax a reaction from her. Sliding his lips gently across her mouth, he slanted his head a little to the side. Without haste, he inhaled her scent and tasted her skin.

She was rigid beneath him, not moving at all: neither to push him away nor to pull him closer. But he knew how to elicit reactions from women, even from a woman who believed sex to be a painful and dirty undertaking—she wouldn't remain frozen like this for long.

Slowly, Nico brought his hand to her neck, sliding it to her nape. His fingers pushed up into her hair, while his thumb caressed the soft skin below her ear. Her pulse beat against his thumb as loudly as a drum. He sensed her tremble under his touch, yet she didn't turn her head to sever the contact.

"Oriana," he whispered against her mouth, before he parted his lips and licked his tongue against the seam of her lips.

A gasp escaped her.

Combing his hand through her hair and in the process disturbing some of the pins that held her coiffure up, he slanted his lips over her mouth, licking over it again. Under light pressure, she parted her lips. She finally understood what he wanted. Or had she simply wanted to take a breath? It didn't matter, because all he could think of was the warm and moist cavern he now explored. With gentle and measured strokes, he delved into her mouth, ever so softly licking over her teeth, before touching her tongue.

A bolt of lightning charged through him, turning his insides into an inferno in an instant. A groan came over his lips before he could stop it. Just like he couldn't stop another bodily reaction: after having been semi-erect ever since entering the room, his cock swelled to its full size, the blood pumping into it bringing it near bursting. His eager appendage pushed against the flap of his trousers, pressing into the buttons. He could only hope that the thread with which the buttons were sewn was strong enough, or he would burst from his trousers and make a fool of himself.

Trying to push away those thoughts, he captured her mouth more fiercely now, kissing her with more passion and determination. To his surprise there was no resistance. This was easier than he'd imagined.

Sighing, he allowed his hands to roam her body. As one of them reached the round swell of her breast and cupped it, Oriana ripped her mouth from his.

A split second later, a sharp pain in his foot made him jump back. Shocked, he stared at her. Oriana had driven the heel of her slipper into his foot.

"How dare you?!" she cried out.

Anger charged through him.

~ ~ ~

Oriana saw the fury blazing from Nico's eyes and instinctively shrank back. His eyes darkened and his jaw clenched.

To her utter shock and dismay, she'd enjoyed his kiss. Or maybe she'd been so surprised by it that she'd been unable to react the way a lady would—with indifference. But when she'd felt his hand on her breast, her brain had suddenly started working again, and she'd done the only thing she could: defend herself.

Narrowing his eyes, Nico approached. "Oh, I dare even more, my sweet wife!"

Suddenly afraid, she froze. She'd unleashed a wild beast in him. Now he would truly hurt her! Before, he would have simply taken her dignity, now he would do much worse. Her heart beating into her throat, she squeezed her eyes shut, not wanting to see what was coming.

A moment later, she felt herself lifted up, then she heard dishes and cutlery crash onto the floor. When he deposited her on the table, she steeled herself for her fate: he would take her right here on the table. She wouldn't even get a bed to cushion her back, instead he'd use her like a common whore. Oh, the indignity!

"No!" she cried out, but Nico didn't stop.

He pushed her skirts up to her waist. Then she felt his hand on her drawers. He ripped them, laying her bare to his view. Shame flooded her. Nobody had ever seen her like this.

"Oh God, you're beautiful." His voice sounded anything but angry—it sounded reverent.

Her eyes flew open. She'd expected to see him opening his trousers to take out his manhood so he could do what men did, but instead she saw him look at the place between her legs, legs he now spread wider.

"And I'm sure you taste as beautiful."

Before she understood what he meant by his words, he sank his head between her legs and brought his lips to her sex. For a long moment, she was frozen in disbelief. What he was doing was impossible. Maybe she had fainted so she wouldn't have to face what was happening to her.

She sensed him inhale sharply, pressing his face into the triangle of hair that guarded her woman's place. It was really happening. She hadn't fainted.

When she felt warm air blow against her, she

realized that he was kissing her there. Kissing a place that was unthinkable. Forbidden. Her friend Ilaria had never mentioned her husband doing anything of the sort. Surely, this was not done!

Oriana was about to protest, trying to lift herself up from her lying position, when his fingers parted her female folds and something warm and moist swiped against them.

"Ohhhhh!" she sighed.

Nico was licking her with his tongue! It was outrageous, but she couldn't gather the strength to push him away, despite the fact that his hands weren't holding her down. He was using no force on her, his fingers too busy caressing her instead. She could easily push him off her and free herself. So why didn't she? Why was she allowing him to do this to her? To kiss her in such a scandalous way?

As if it had been turned off, her mind gave no answer to her questions. Instead her body dictated her reaction. Like a wanton woman, she moaned, her body writhing against his mouth and tongue, her pelvis tilting toward him to achieve a closer connection.

Her body was aflame, burning from the inside out. At the same time, her nipples were chafing against her corset, begging to be freed, yet there was no way of doing so. But she needed relief. Without thinking, she rubbed her palms over her breasts, cupping and squeezing them as much as was possible through the fabric. It wasn't enough to give her any sense of relief, so she allowed her fingers to trail higher, ignoring the little voice in her head that called her "wanton" and instead touched the part of her skin that was exposed. Then she hooked her thumbs underneath the corset and pushed it farther down. Another pull, and her nipples popped over the rim of the corset. Cool air blew against them, making the hard tips even harder.

She moaned in response. At the same time, Nico licked with more intensity and pressed harder against her exposed flesh. She felt liquid pool there. With it, embarrassment swept through her. What was she doing? How could she allow him to see her like this, to touch her like this?

And on the dining table of all places! That thought sent a shockwave through her body. What if one of the servants entered and saw them?

"We can't..." she stammered.

Instead of an answer, Nico moved his position and licked higher up, reaching a spot where her heartbeat pulsed violently. He licked over it, sending a charge through her body as if she'd been hit by lightning.

"Ohhh!" she cried out, pleasure racing through her.

No, she didn't want him to stop now. She wanted more of this, more of what he was doing right now. Whatever he was doing. She had no words for it. But it didn't stop her from begging, "More. Oh God, more!"

She knew there had to be more of this kind of sensation, this joy that traveled through her body and made her toss her inhibitions out the window and into the canals below. There was something she couldn't put a name to that was just beyond her reach. Something wonderful, something pleasurable. Her body knew it as if it was a primal instinct. And her body now drove her toward it, ignoring all manners and decorum.

Nico was doing this to her. Her husband was giving her something she'd never experienced. Was this what married couples really did? Then why had Ilaria made it sound like it was all pain and shame? The shame she could understand, because even now she felt ashamed at her lusty behavior, like that of a common trollop and not the lady she was. But there was no pain. Nico's fingers stroked her gently as if he knew what she needed, where she wanted to be touched. Indeed he seemed to know better than she did, because his caresses reached places before she even knew she needed his touch there.

Just like he now stroked along her folds while his tongue licked over the small bundle of nerves that was so sensitive she felt she might explode any moment. But whenever she thought it would happen, Nico pulled back and decreased the pressure. Over and over he did this, varying the intensity with which he licked and stroked her, as if he wanted to hold off the inevitable.

Oriana felt one finger probe at the entrance to her body, sliding between the moist folds. Instinctively, she spread her legs wider and pulled her knees up so they pointed toward the ceiling. She didn't care that no lady would ever expose herself like this—all she cared about was that she gave him better access to her sex.

Nico's next groan reverberated through her, and at the same time his finger slid into her. The invasion was foreign at first, her muscles clamping around him instantly. Before she could decide whether she liked what he did, the pressure on her center of pleasure intensified and she let out an involuntary moan.

She barely noticed how Nico's finger moved in and out of her, because the pleasure from him licking and sucking her drove every sane thought out of her mind.

Her hands went back to her breasts, strumming her nipples while her hips bucked against Nico's mouth, encouraging him to go faster. Her chest heaved, and small beads of sweat built on her face and neck. She ignored them and instead squeezed her breasts harder.

"Yes, yes, yes," she chanted without thinking.

Who was this lusty woman who'd taken over her body? Who was controlling her now? Because for certain it wasn't the studious young woman who'd never shown any interest in men.

A grumble came from Nico. "Yes, my wanton wife!"

Then everything changed. Nico sucked her sensitive flesh into his mouth and pressed his lips together. At the same time, his finger drove deep and hard into her. With a cry, she exploded. Waves of pleasure raced through her body, threatening to incinerate her. But no flames consumed her body, instead she felt as if floating on a cloud. Weightless. Without any thoughts, without any worries in the world.

Her vision blurred, and she realized that tears were running down her cheeks.

When she finally floated down back, her limbs felt boneless. She was overcome with emotions, but of one thing she was certain: she wanted more of this, and more of Nico.

Nico's head lifted and he looked at her. Concern spread over his face when he noticed her tears. His hand reached to wipe one off her cheek.

Then, with a pained expression, he turned on his heels and stormed out of the room.

"Nico!" But he was already gone.

14

She would never survive this. This much was certain.

Rose listened to the sounds of the shower in the en-suite bathroom and felt her body heat rise with every second that passed.

The room Quinn had led her into was a large

bedroom, luxuriously furnished with a King sized bed and comfortable looking furniture in the sitting area in front of a fireplace. Yet instead of using the furniture, she paced about the room.

This was not good.

What had she been thinking, accepting his outrageous condition? If she slept with him, she would never be able to keep her emotional distance from him. She would want more, feel that closeness again that they had once shared. And she would want to confess. Tell him what had really happened. Everything. And it would get her killed.

When the floorboards creaked shortly after the water was turned off, she knew her short reprieve was over. Quinn demanded what was due to him, and she had no choice but to do what he wanted.

Slowly she turned and looked toward the door to the bathroom. Shock made her freeze in place. He hadn't bothered wearing a robe. A towel that barely covered his groin was slung low around his hips, the ends tucked in so haphazardly, they threatened to come loose if he moved.

Her mouth went dry at the sight of his chiseled abs and the defined muscles of his chest, arms, and legs.

Her breath caught, and she quickly averted her eyes.

A moment later, the soft trickle of his voice reached her. "Now, now, Rose. You've seen me wearing less than this."

Maybe, but he hadn't looked like that back then. Clearly the year he'd spent on the battlefield with Wellington's troupes had made him leaner, more defined. And stronger. She chanced another look at his thighs, admiring the smooth skin that covered sinew and muscle, creating a physique that would have put any Greek god to shame.

Swallowing away the lump in her throat, she allowed her eyes to travel higher. It did no good to show weakness now. She couldn't let him know how much he affected her. After all, this wasn't about the fabulous sex they would have shortly. It was about power, about who would come out ahead. And if she admitted that the mere sight of him made her weak in the knees, she might as well throw in the towel now.

Collecting all her courage, she raised her head to meet his gaze and forced a nonchalant shrug. "I've seen a lot of men naked."

When she noticed him narrow his eyes, she added, "More than I can count."

A low growl issued from his chest, and for some strange reason, which she didn't want to examine at present, it filled her with satisfaction.

"Don't think you can play me, Rose. Those days are over."

Quinn took a step toward her. Instinct dictated that she retreat, but her mind overrode her body's reaction. Retreat would only make this worse. She wasn't his prey. He would be hers.

"I wouldn't think of it. This is a business arrangement, nothing else."

And to make it obvious to him, she pulled her top from her jeans and yanked it over her head, tossing it to the nearby couch. The bra she wore was transparent. Had she known that he wanted to collect payment immediately, she would have worn something less enticing.

"I'm assuming you want to fuck now," she said,

getting busy with the button on her jeans. She'd always hated that word, fuck, but she forced herself to use it, showing him how little this meant to her, even if she couldn't convince herself of it.

Only when his hand captured hers, stopping her from lowering her zipper, did she realize that he had moved. Startled, she lifted her head and collided with his gaze.

"I think you're forgetting one thing: I'm in charge here. I decide when you get undressed and how. Are we clear on that?"

His voice was a low rumble, but she could barely concentrate on it, because he suddenly stood too close. His scent wrapped around her like a blanket, making it impossible for her to breathe. Little electrical charges seemed to dance on his skin and jump to hers, scorching her.

His hand suddenly came up, sliding underneath her mane, capturing the back of her neck in a firm grip. Effortlessly, he pulled her head closer.

"Do we understand each other... Rose?"

Her heart skipped a beat. Had she imagined it, or had his last word carried the same kind of tenderness as that night she'd become his wife?

She searched his hazel eyes, looking for an answer to her questions, but he gave nothing away. Whatever had been there only a split-second earlier, was gone. Or maybe it was simply an illusion, a trick her tired mind played on her.

That same mind now urged her to give in, to surrender. Maybe it was best that way. After two hundred years she was tired of running away, of hiding. She had to do this for Blake, because she had promised Charlotte, she told herself.

With a sigh, she brought her body flush against his. "I understand. Go ahead, take what you want."

Quinn's lips crushed hers before her last word was out. He wasn't tender, not the way he'd been that night in London, and she was glad for it. Tenderness would have crushed her courage and crumbled her resolve to guard her heart. Yet his kiss had another effect: it stoked her desire.

His lips plundered, explored, and demanded. They were both hard and soft as they slanted over her mouth, urging her to surrender. Her skin sizzled under the impact, and his masculine breath only fanned the flames in her body.

Forgetting her plan to remain uninvolved, she slung her arms around his neck and parted her lips under the imploring command of his tongue. A rush of heat charged through her, setting her ablaze, robbing her of the ability to think. When his tongue foraged into her, invading her mouth, she felt her brain disintegrate into a gooey mess.

She felt his silky tongue slide against her teeth, coaxing her to respond to him. Without thinking, she did. With the same perfect rhythm they had danced in the ballrooms of London, their tongues now twirled to a music she could sense reverberating through her entire body. The melody carried her away, cradled her in safety, yet hurtled her toward the inevitable.

Underneath her bra, her nipples chafed as he pressed her harder against his rock-hard chest. The ache was unbearable, but relief was nowhere in sight, because Quinn seemed to have no intention of letting go of her mouth yet to devote his energies to her aching breasts.

One hand was still at her nape to assure she didn't

escape the devastating talent of his mouth, the other one palmed her backside as he rubbed his groin against her sex. She felt the hard outline of his cock, but the towel still clung to his hips, preventing a closer connection.

With one swift move, she pulled on it and freed him from it.

A startled gasp was his answer. Then his kiss intensified as if he wanted to punish her for what she'd done. Did he really think he could silence her, take the lead in this? She would show him that she would not be the timid playmate he had once had, the one who'd looked up to him with wonder in her eyes. No, she would take what she wanted.

Digging her nails into his backside, she ground her sex against his hard-on.

Quinn ripped his mouth from hers. "Fuck, Rose!" His eyes were red as he glared at her. "I told you—"

"Fuck you, Quinn! You think I'm still the virgin who's going to obediently spread her legs for you? If you wanna fuck, then we'll do it my way!"

Before he could reply, she reached behind her, releasing the clasp of her bra, sliding the irritating garment off her body.

His gaze instantly shot to her breasts.

"And what way is that, Rose?" he ground out, the tips of his fangs peeking from between his lips.

Her mouth salivated at the sight. She'd never before considered the view of extended fangs sexy. But now, the way he glared at her, it suddenly weakened her knees.

"Well, it sure isn't the way you did it back then!"

His eyes narrowed. Well, now she'd done it. He looked furious. He growled low and dark.

"I know what you're doing. It's not working."

She lifted her chin. "What do you think I'm going?"

"Don't play daft! You think by insulting me, can get out of your obligation. How stupid do you think I am? I'm going to have you. Right now. There's no way out."

It wasn't at all what she'd been doing, but there was no point in correcting him. All she'd wanted was to get it over with, with as little emotional involvement as possible. And that meant as quickly as possible, without any drawn-out foreplay.

Before her eyes, his hands turned into claws. In vampire speed, he ripped her jeans to shreds, tossing the destroyed garment to the floor. Her bikini panties followed.

She should feel at least a little scared, yet no such feeling took hold. Instead, her nipples tightened and a steady trickle of moisture made its way to the outer lips of her sex.

~ ~ ~

Quinn took a steadying breath, hoping Rose didn't notice that he was practically drooling. She was even more beautiful than he remembered her. Her body was more mature, her hips a little rounder than that night he'd taken her virginity. And her breasts were fuller too. Had the pregnancy done that to her? Was that why she was even more feminine now?

Her skin was still alabaster, her hard nipples a dark tan color, and her lips a deep red. He smelled the scent of her arousal and noticed the dew that glistened on the curls that guarded her sex. As his eyes roamed over her naked body, his anger dissipated. His claws turned back to fingers, but his

117

fangs remained extended. The state of his fangs had nothing to do with anger, and everything to do with lust and desire.

Knowing how close he was to grabbing her and pressing her against the wall, fucking her standing up, he balled his hands into fists. No, he wouldn't allow her to control him like this. He would fuck her just like any other woman, and after it was over, he would realize that there was nothing special about it, that sex with her would be just like sex with any other woman.

"Lie down."

Her lips opened as if wanting to protest.

"Now, Rose!"

Maybe she had seen the determination in his eyes, or maybe the fact that he had shredded her pants had finally made it clear to her that he wasn't joking, but she complied with his request and stretched out on the bed.

She looked like a kitten, her beautiful body contrasted against the dark red sheets, her blond hair fanned out around her like a halo. One leg angled, she made an attempt at hiding her exposed sex from him. Despite the coldness she'd displayed, he had to wonder whether this meant anything to her.

She'd made it clear that she'd seen many men naked. It had been her way of telling him that she'd slept with countless men since he'd deflowered her. Flaunting this fact was an attempt at angering him, for sure. It shouldn't matter, yet it did. Knowing that other men had touched her, been inside her, pleasured her, made his blood boil.

His anger was back in an instant. Maybe it was better this way. Maybe the anger he felt inside him would prevent him from making this into more than it was: pure sex. An itch he needed to scratch.

Determined to prove to himself that she meant nothing to him anymore, he lowered himself onto the bed, pushing her legs apart in the process. He noticed how she closed her eyes. He didn't care. If she didn't want to look at him, it didn't matter. She'd gawked at him earlier, and those few seconds when her eyes had roamed his half naked body had given him some satisfaction. If she wanted to deny it now that there were still remnants of desire between them, then he'd allow it.

Smelling her arousal more intensely, now that her legs were spread before him, reminded him of how he'd feasted on her that night, how he'd enjoyed licking her, drinking her nectar. But he wouldn't do it tonight. This wasn't lovemaking. It was simply sex. If only he could convince his body of this fact.

Quinn moved between her thighs, centering himself over her sex. Without a word, he drove his aching cock into her, pushing deep.

Her eyes shot open, her lips parting on a moan.

Oh, fuck, he was so screwed!

Her slick warmth welcomed him home, her interior muscles gripping him like a tight fist, holding him there like a prisoner. With one single thrust, he'd sealed his fate. It couldn't be. It was impossible, but just being inside her, without even moving, without doing anything, he was aware of the power she still had over him. The power she would always have over him.

"Rose," he whispered, unable to stop his lips from moving.

His hand came up, wanting to caress her cheek, but he quickly suppressed the urge. This wasn't lovemaking, he repeated his mantra. No emotions, no feelings should be involved. He had to remain unaffected. Maybe once he'd found release, he would feel differently. Maybe then, he would see her as just another woman.

Determined to destroy whatever power she had over him, he withdrew from her tight sheath, then plunged back in. It shouldn't matter to him what she felt, whether she enjoyed this or didn't, yet he found himself watching her for signs of pleasure. Every time she let a moan or a sigh emerge, his chest swelled with pride and his cock throbbed in anticipation. He sensed how he adjusted his rhythm to her breathing, how he longed for her hands to touch him.

But her hands remained at her sides. Why didn't she touch him? He glanced at them and noticed how her nails were digging into the sheets, slicing them.

His head whipped back to her face, and he saw how she pulled her lower lip between her teeth, clearly trying not to cry out.

Fuck, pride be damned! "Touch me, Rose!" he commanded. "Do it!"

She instantly released her lip, a surprised look on her face. But moments later, her hands let go of the sheets and she placed them on his chest, stroking him.

He expelled a shaky breath, followed by a moan. Wherever she touched him, he was on fire. There was no use in denying it: her hands were magical. They conjured up memories of a life long gone, of secret kisses and stolen moments, of clandestine meetings and frantic touches. Of a forbidden love.

Everything felt like the first time. Her hands were just as soft as then, yet the shy hands of his virgin

Rose were replaced by the experienced touch of a woman who knew what a man needed. Her nails dug into him, demanding, he'd increase his tempo and pound harder into her. Back then, he hadn't been able to do that for fear of hurting her, but today he could drive into her as hard as he wanted, and she would welcome him. Her body was as indestructible as his, yet as pliable as ever.

"More!" she demanded, pulling him closer with her legs wrapped around him.

He had no objections. Riding her hard and fast was just what he needed.

The shy virgin from two centuries earlier had vanished. Quinn couldn't say that he regretted that fact, because the woman who now writhed underneath him, whose body gave him such pleasure, was everything he'd ever dreamed of and more. She'd blossomed into the perfect lover.

Passionate and wild, she tantalized him with unscripted moans and sighs. Her body's reactions to his powerful thrusts were immediate and raw. And with every slide into her silken softness, he lost himself one bit more. Every second of their bodies dancing in perfect harmony, brought him closer to ecstasy. Release beckoned, but he pulled back, slowed down. He couldn't allow this to be over yet. It was too good to stop.

So he endured the torture she dealt him: one lash at a time, one slide, one push. And maybe just one kiss. What would be the harm in that?

On the next thrust, he lowered his head to hers, brought his lips down on her mouth and kissed her. It was different this time, not as angry. She greeted him with passion, slid her tongue against his invitingly, asking him to take her. She didn't have to tell him twice. This time when he invaded her mouth, he did so knowing that she wanted him and that it had nothing to do with the bargain they'd struck. He felt it.

The knowledge catapulted him over the edge. Without warning, his balls tightened, the pressure in them becoming unbearable. Fire shot into his cock, exploding from the tip.

Rose gasped into his mouth.

"Oh, God!" he ground out, ripping his lips from hers.

The waves of his orgasm hit him and whipped him like an Atlantic storm tossing a canoe in the surf. Then another wave crashed, and he realized that this one wasn't coming from him. It was Rose. Her muscles convulsed around his iron rod, clamping down on him so he couldn't leave, couldn't withdraw from her moist cavern. Not that he had any intention of doing so.

He continued riding her, his thrusts slowing and adjusting to her spasms. Captured between her thighs, he moved in and out of her, prolonging the pleasure that coursed through his veins.

When he finally rolled off her, he heard her exhale next to him. He turned his body to face her, angling his elbow and resting his head on his palm.

Maybe they could repair what had gone wrong between them. What he'd just experienced with her had been perfect. He couldn't just throw that away.

"Tell me what happened back then," he said softly, stroking his knuckles along her neck.

She evaded his gaze. "We had an agreement. I'll tell you once Blake is out of danger."

At her refusal, his heart beat faster, but he wasn't willing to give up trying. "Why not? Please tell me, Rose. After you got turned, why did you let me believe you were dead?"

Her mouth tightened. "It doesn't matter."

Quinn shot up to sit. "It matters to me. I loved you, Rose! I thought you felt the same back then."

He stared at the empty fireplace, waiting for her answer, knowing what he wanted to hear: a confession of her love. Then whatever else she would tell him wouldn't matter. Whatever reasons she'd had for never coming to see him, he would understand. If only she'd loved him. Even if she didn't love him anymore. He could live with that. At least he would try.

"I told you I'll explain everything later. But Blake is more important right now. He's in danger and—"

He lifted a hand, stopping her. The knowledge that she was hiding something from him solidified in his stomach and formed tiny painful knots. "I understand," he ground out. "You love Blake more than you ever loved me. I hope you two are gonna be very happy together."

Catapulting from the bed, he snatched the towel from the floor.

"Where are you going?"

He didn't turn but stalked to the door, wrapping the towel around his hips in the process. "Where do you think I'm going, Rose? To my room. We might still be married, but we're not a couple anymore. We never truly were."

The words almost choked his airways off and delivered a painful stab into his heart as if somebody were driving a knife into it. God, how much he'd wanted to have her in his arms, listen to her heartbeat as she slept, cradle her, feel her breath ghosting over his skin. And then, at sunset, wake up with her, feel her stir in his arms, her warm body molded to his, her sweet bottom tucked into his groin.

How many days had he dreamt of it? How many times had he wished for the impossible, for a life with Rose? And even now as he slammed the door shut behind him, he knew those dreams hadn't died. He was irrevocably in love with Rose. For two hundred years he'd kept the love for her alive, and tonight, it had been reaffirmed. She was still his, the wife he'd claimed that fateful night, the woman he couldn't forget. The one who'd spoiled him for all others.

His plan of purging his love for Rose had failed.

What was he supposed to do now?

15

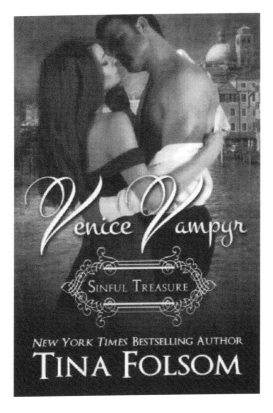

Lorenzo had planned on arriving at his new home just after sunset, however his friends had thwarted his efforts to take possession of his new residence by calling another meeting to discuss more details about the acquisition of the remaining twenty-six homes on the square block. He'd only listened half-heartedly, eager to inspect his new place. After all, he'd bought it sight unseen. He'd never set foot inside. For all he knew, the place was in shambles.

However, the solicitor had assured him the property was habitable and only needed some cleaning. It didn't matter much to Lorenzo. He was going to change the interior anyway. For starters, hidden exits would have to be incorporated into the layout of the home, and once the house between his and that of the brothers Dante and Raphael was in vampire hands, connecting tunnels would be built between the homes. Of course, these were not to be true tunnels, but covered walkways, above ground. Any attempt to dig beneath the level of the canals would result in immediate flooding. But such walkways would serve their purpose, allowing them to move around during the day.

It was well past midnight by the time Lorenzo reached the front door of his new home and turned the key. The smell that greeted him wasn't what he'd expected from a vacant house. It was welcoming, instantly feeling like a home. And he immediately realized why: somewhere in the house, a fire was burning in a fireplace. He was not alone.

Dropping his traveling bag in the foyer, he inhaled deeply, taking in the various scents of the house: smoke, soap, dust, and mold. And another very faint smell of something entirely unexpected.

A smile curled around his lips. Dante and Nico were the best. They knew him too well, and there was no doubt in his mind about what they'd gotten him as a housewarming gift. Emphasis on the "warming."

Lorenzo followed the alluring scent upstairs and trailed it along the corridor. In front of one door, he stopped and inhaled again. Yes, his gift was right behind this door, waiting for him. His ears captured every sound, but it was quiet behind the door except for the crackling of the fire.

Quietly, he turned the door knob and eased the door open, sliding inside the nearly dark room. Only the low fire in the fireplace provided some light, but Lorenzo's superior night vision didn't need bright light to make out the outlines of his present.

There, in the entirely feminine chamber, which at one time must have belonged to the lady of the house, a young woman slumbered under the sheets. Her dark hair fanned out like a halo around her porcelain face, her lips slightly parted, her breath beckoning him to approach.

He wondered what color her eyes were. Maybe as dark as her thick lashes, which seemed so long they caressed her cheeks.

Why had Nico and Dante kept him so long when they knew this enthralling beauty was waiting for him? It was inexcusable to let a woman like her wait and not give her the attention she deserved. He had every intention of making it up to her.

Without making a sound, Lorenzo took off his cloak and dropped it on a nearby chair before divesting himself of his shirt. When he opened the top button of his breeches, he realized that he was already hard. He stripped himself of his trousers and shoes, placing them next to the rest of his clothing. Then he looked back at the sleeping woman in his bed and touched his cock, trying to ease some of the tension.

His arousal was heavy and unstoppable. As much as he enjoyed looking at her, what he wanted even more was to touch her. And then wake her. Fuck her. Bite her. Not necessarily in that order.

Lorenzo released his erection and lifted the coverlet, revealing more of the woman's body. She wore a nightrail which revealed more than it concealed. The thin lilac fabric was virtually transparent, putting her dark nipples on display. With every breath, her full breasts rose and pressed the little buds against the fabric, the chafing action seemingly turning them hard.

He licked his lips at the sight and slid onto the bed. His eyes continued scanning her body, moving over her slender waist and further down. A dark thatch of hair shone through the fabric where her thighs met. Slightly parted, her sex was open to be explored if he chose to do so.

Her nightgown had ridden up, revealing a creamy thigh, the skin pink and unblemished, toned, yet not muscular. Surely, those thighs would grip him tightly when he thrust into her. Those were not the thighs of a virgin.

Lorenzo forced his gaze upwards again, past her tempting cunt and her luscious breasts to that little hollow at the base of her neck. Graceful, elegant. She was all that and more. The long column of her neck fairly screamed to be bitten, and her ears were petite and beautifully shaped, ready to be nibbled on.

He had to hand it to Nico and Dante: they knew what he liked in a woman. And this time, they'd outdone themselves. He would have to thank them for this thoughtful gift—later. After he'd devoured her and had his fill of her. And he wasn't going to wait a second longer, whether she woke up while he touched her or not. In fact, he liked the idea of her waking up only once he was thrusting inside her.

He would arouse her while she was asleep, then take her and continue when she awoke in his arms, surprised and delighted at his mastery over her body.

Lorenzo allowed his fingers to lightly glide over her breasts, making the fabric rub more tightly against her nipples. Even through the fabric, he sensed the heat in her body and the sensitivity of her skin to his touch. Without haste, he explored her. His eyes mapped her body for a later conquest while his hands forged ahead to touch her lush curves. Her breasts were firm and sitting high on her chest, evidence of a young and well-tended body. As he squeezed one of the round globes lightly, a soft breath rushed past her lips and bounced against him. The taste of mint and vanilla engulfed him, making him pause for a moment.

Mint and vanilla—the scents he associated with innocence when he knew that the woman in his bed was far from innocent. His friends had bought her for the night to please him with her body. And while she didn't look as if she'd been cheap, she was no innocent, but a seductress as sophisticated as they came. Her nightgown spoke to that effect. But as much as he liked the gown, it had to go.

Lorenzo wanted to feast his eyes on her skin, her curves, her sex. He wanted nothing impeding his mouth and hands, no barriers, not even as thin as the fabric of her gown. Three purple ribbons held the nightgown together in the front now that he looked at it more closely. In fact, it appeared the gown wasn't really as much of a gown as it was a robe meant to be worn over something else.

Had she waited for him only dressed in this flimsy

robe, wanting him to simply untie those three ribbons before he'd throw her on the bed and drive his shaft into her? Had that been her intention? A present for which he would have simply had to untie three purple ribbons? How fitting.

As he released the top ribbon, the valley between her breasts was laid bare. He couldn't help himself: he had to taste her. His head dipped between her breasts, and his lips brushed against her soft skin as he placed a gentle kiss on the spot. When he inhaled, he scented the soap she'd used only recently. It was the same scent he'd smelled upon entering the home. It appeared she'd bathed here. He appreciated the gesture. He liked a clean woman, and if she'd bathed, it could only mean that she would be more than happy for him to taste her beautiful cunt, something he was more than eager to do.

But he shouldn't get ahead of himself. First, he needed to unwrap his present completely and not act like a little boy who couldn't wait to get to what was underneath, tearing the wrapping in the process. No, he wanted to peel her out of it, reveal inch by glorious inch of her body to his hungry gaze. He wanted to revel in the anticipation, because he knew he'd climax so much harder if only he'd allow himself to wait until the last possible moment.

And she was a beauty to behold. When Lorenzo untied the last ribbon, he peeled each side of the gauzy robe to its side and laid her bare. Her breasts were as beautiful as he'd imagined, but when his gaze traveled over her flat stomach and down to where her womanly scent emanated, his heart nearly stopped.

Her sex was guarded by a neatly trimmed triangle of dark hair, but it was shorter and slimmer than what he was used to from other women. She'd shaped it into a long stripe, a little wider at the top, but slimming toward the bottom, almost as if it was an arrow pointing the way.

Not that he needed any directions.

His hand followed the arrow of hair and slid between her parted legs. Her sex was damp, either from her recent bath or maybe, already, from her arousal. Lorenzo glanced back at her face, but her eyes were closed and her breathing was even.

He smiled, liking the fact that she was still asleep, giving him the opportunity to explore at his leisure. Again, he dipped his head to her breasts and licked his tongue over one hard nipple. He loved the hard nipple grazing his tongue and took another lick before he closed his lips around it and sucked.

But his hand wasn't idle either. He rubbed one finger against her female folds, feeling the moisture spread under his ministrations. She shifted under him, and he realized it was to open her legs wider and give him better access. He thanked her by sucking her nipple harder before he released it and moved to the other breast where he unleashed the same treatment.

Whether it was him sucking her breasts, or his finger stroking her softly, her cunt released more moisture. He swept it up with the pad of his finger and stroked upwards, finding the little bundle of flesh that was now peeking from its hood. He slid his moist finger over it and simultaneously heard her moan out a breath.

She was responding to him in her sleep. Uninhibited, just as he loved it. Her aroma drifted into his nostrils, making his cock throb in anticipation. Soon, he promised himself. As soon as he'd tasted her.

Lorenzo slid down and settled between her thighs. As he spread them further, he opened up her cunt to his view. The beautiful pink flesh glistened in the light from the fireplace as if flames danced on its surface. He lowered his lips to her sex and lapped against it. When her juices hit the back of his tongue, he inhaled sharply and closed his eyes. By God, she tasted like paradise.

16

He'd given Marcus instructions to take care of the two newcomers, and now Cain closed the door to Faye's suite behind him, flipping the lock. His gaze traveled to Faye who stood near the fireplace and didn't move.

He didn't care that there was *king business* waiting

for him. What he was about to do was more important than ruling a kingdom.

"Thank you for helping those two vampires," she murmured.

He walked to her with steady steps although his heart was thundering. "I want you to know that I didn't do it in order to get you into my bed."

Faye laughed softly and motioned to the bed. "That's my bed, not yours."

"Same difference." Having reached her, he braced his hands at either side of her head. "If I remember well, it never mattered much to me which bed I slept in as long as you were with me." At least that much he knew from his dreams.

"And sometimes it didn't even matter to you whether it was a bed." She glanced down at the bearskin rug at her feet.

Had they made love there before?

"Why don't you show me what you like best?" he suggested.

Her lips came closer, and her breath bounced against his mouth. "You know what I like best."

Cain wished he could remember, but no memory was forthcoming. So he did the only thing he could. He captured her lips and kissed her. Her lips yielded to him, parting at the slightest pressure, a soft sigh escaping her mouth, while one of her hands slid to his nape, sending a shiver down his spine and into his tailbone. A corresponding bolt traveled to his groin and ignited him there.

He'd hoped it would be like this ever since the moment she'd appeared in his dreams, but he'd never expected Faye's passion to engulf him so fully that he lost all sense of reality. This could only be a dream;

nothing could feel so good in real life. Yet holding Faye in his arms and devouring her lips like a man dying of thirst felt more real than all of the dreams he'd had about her combined.

He felt his heart roar to life as if it had been dormant since the beginning of time. It beat against her chest, providing the echo to Faye's heartbeat. Just as rapidly as his, her heart thundered inside her ribcage trying to escape. His hand moved south to capture it, to finally feel her warm flesh in his palm. Soft flesh greeted him, filling his hand to its capacity. His thumb stroked over her peak, feeling it harden under his caress. But the fabric of her summer dress was still in his way, still preventing him from making contact with her skin.

Cain ripped his mouth from her, panting heavily. "Oh, God, Faye!" He gazed into her eyes. They were heavy-lidded, the passion in them undisguised. It made him hungry just looking at her.

He squeezed her breast in his palm, then captured her other one with his other hand. Faye leaned her head back against the wall and moaned.

"It's not enough," he ground out and took hold of the fabric. Without thinking, he ripped the top of her dress in two, exposing her breasts.

Faye gasped, her eyes widening in surprise.

Cain dropped his gaze, drinking in the sight. She wore no bra, and her generous breasts spilled into his waiting hands. The contact of skin on skin made his cock throb uncontrollably, thickening further.

"God damn it, Faye, take my cock out before I explode!" he ordered before he dropped his head to her breasts and captured one nipple in his mouth.

He sucked on the delicious bud and licked his

tongue over it, when he finally felt her hands on his pants, popping the button open. Then one hand pressed against the length of his shaft, while the other pulled the zipper down.

He felt release when the tightness of his pants made way for cool air as she pulled his pants and boxer briefs lower so they rested mid-thigh. Impatient, he ground his cock against her hands.

"Cain, my love!" she murmured and wrapped one hand around his iron-hard erection and slid down on him.

Her nipple popped from his mouth. "Fuck!" If she continued to stroke him like this, he would spill in her hand in three seconds flat. "Don't!" He breathed heavily, pulling himself from her grip.

"What's wrong?"

"What's wrong?" he repeated. "Faye, I'm going to come instantly if you do that to me."

"But I'm barely touching you."

He stared into her eyes, bringing his head closer to hers. "You're like a new woman to me. As if I've never touched you before. This might be over faster than we both want."

Her finger retraced his lips. "In that case we'll just have to do it again and again until we're both satisfied with the outcome."

Cain smiled at her. "So you're not gonna toss me out on my ass if I don't get it right the first time?" Because for him, this would be the first time he made love to her. He had nothing to compare it with other than his dreams. Yet Faye would compare him to the old Cain.

"My love," she murmured, shaking her head as if to reprimand him. "You've never gotten it wrong.

You know my body better than I do."

He grinned. "Well, in that case…" He slipped his shirt over his head and tossed it on the floor. Then he took hold of her dress again and ripped the remainder in two.

His eyes wandered lower. "You're wearing panties today." In his last dream, she'd been bare.

"That's because I wasn't expecting this."

Cain clicked his tongue. "You should always be expecting it. Day and night. Because a woman like you should have her legs spread and my cock inside her twenty-four-seven."

Faye tossed him a coquettish look. "Then why are you still talking?"

"Good point," he acknowledged and took her lips again.

He remembered the dream where he'd taken her against the wall, but this wasn't how he wanted to take her for the first time. He needed her underneath him.

Kissing her hard, he lifted her into his arms and brought her down onto the bearskin rug before he released her, kicked his shoes off, and made quick work of his pants and socks. He wanted nothing to impede his movements.

Faye's hands reached for him to draw him down to her and he complied, sliding between her spread legs. Only her tiny panties now covered the precious spot at the apex of her thighs, yet didn't prevent the scent of her arousal from spreading in the room. His nostrils flared when they filled with the tantalizing aroma.

With his knuckles he rubbed against the fabric, making her jolt. "Easy, baby," he murmured. "I'll give you everything you need." Or die trying. But he wouldn't be rushed. He wanted to explore her, to get to know her body, to feast his eyes on her.

Had he really had a woman like her before when he'd still been the old Cain? When he'd had a memory? What a lucky son-of-a-bitch he must have been to have called a woman like Faye his own.

The knowledge that nobody had touched her during his absence filled him with satisfaction. And for that he would reward her now, so she would know how much he appreciated her loyalty and faithfulness.

His fingers slid under the fabric of her delicate panties.

"Hmm," she hummed, licking her lips and arching her back.

Encouraged by her receptiveness, he explored her moist flesh. She was soft and warm, her female folds drenched with her juices, her knees at an angle now to give him better access. By her reaction he knew that he'd done this to her many times. But for him it was all new. Exciting, thrilling. To touch a woman for the first time and learn what she liked, to give her pleasure, was an experience nobody could ever repeat. That he had this chance now, that he was able to start all over again with Faye, he was grateful for.

Cain bathed his fingers in her wetness before he dove farther south. Impatient to get a taste of what her muscles felt like when they would squeeze his cock, he probed at her entrance and drove his finger into her.

A gasp came from her. "Cain!" she panted. "Please, don't tease me."

Did she want more than just one finger? Already

now she felt too tight for even one digit. Once he thrust into her with his cock, she would milk him in an instant.

"I'm not gonna rush this. You'll have to wait for my cock just a little while longer." Despite the fact that he himself could barely wait any longer.

Withdrawing his finger amidst a protesting mewl, he gripped her panties and pulled them down before discarding them on the floor. Finally he could feast his eyes on her. The sight made him salivate. Unable to resist, he lowered his head and brought his mouth to her pussy. His hands clamped over her upper thighs when he heard her moan.

"I haven't even started," Cain murmured, grinning.

"Then start," Faye begged.

She didn't have to tell him twice. He lapped his tongue against her soft female flesh and allowed the flavor to spread. Involuntarily he closed his eyes and let himself fall. Greedily he licked her, explored her, while Faye writhed underneath him, her hips lifting to grind against him, her lips issuing moans and sighs. Sounds of pleasure like the ones he remembered from his dreams echoed in his ears.

Intoxicated by her scent and her taste, he continued licking her, while he released one thigh, only to drive a finger into her quivering slit, so he could concentrate his efforts on a spot farther up. When he swiped his tongue over her swollen clit, she nearly lifted off the rug. He growled, letting her know that he wasn't done yet.

Faye put her hands on his head, caressing the short hair and sensitive scalp, sending a bolt of lust through his body and right down into the tip of his cock. Moisture dripped from its slit, and he knew he couldn't last much longer.

Cain lifted his head from her pussy and looked up. He met her eyes watching him.

"You're so different," she whispered and pulled him to her.

He couldn't let her think that something was different about him, so he gripped her hips and lifted himself over her, adjusted his angle, and plunged into her wet heat.

Faye's eyes closed on impact and a breath rushed from her lungs. "Yes!"

Her cry echoed his own as the sensation of her tight muscles clamping around his erection slammed into him.

"Look at me," Cain demanded.

Her eyes flew open and she pinned him. Slowly, he pulled back from her tight sheath and slid back into her, all the while looking into her eyes. Faye crossed her ankles over his butt and pulled him closer.

"I missed you," she confessed.

"All of me?" He plunged deeper into her, emphasizing his question.

"All of you." Her fingernails dug into his back, urging him to give her more.

Clenching his jaw to ward off his imminent climax, Cain began to thrust. Like a silk glove she enveloped him on every descent, and like a vise she pulled him back on each withdrawal. Her body felt like heaven on earth. Heat suffused his body as if the rays of the sun were shining on him, not burning but warming him, giving him a feeling of belonging.

He'd hoped making love to Faye would be

special, but he hadn't expected it to be as earth shattering as it was. His muscles flexed and his hips worked frantically to deliver thrust after thrust into her intoxicating body. It seemed impossible to think that he'd once called Faye his own and had no memory of it. How could any man forget that he'd been with a woman like her, a woman who made him feel like the most powerful man in the world?

Every sigh and every moan she released fueled his drive to give her more, to show her that he would do everything to give her pleasure, to make her happy. And to keep her safe and never let her go again. And even though his mind had no memory of their prior lovemaking, his body seemed to remember now. His movements seemed to have a mind of their own, adjusting to the demands of her body, coaxing more pleasure from her.

Never for a second did he take his eyes off her face, reveling in the signs of lust and passion that reflected on it, and encouraging him to continue even when his body wanted to give into release. Only when Faye found her release would he grant himself his own. This sign of selflessness took him by surprise, because he hadn't seen this trait in his character before. Was she the one who brought it out in him? Was she the one who made him the man he wanted to be?

The aroma created by their bodies rubbing together filled his nostrils and brought his movements to a more and more frantic pace. Had Faye been human she would have perceived his movements as a mere blur, and the wildness with which he drove into her would have injured her delicate female flesh. But the vampire vixen beneath him had no such limitations. She reacted to him in the same out of control way. Her fingernails had turned into claws and were digging deep into his back, while her hips slammed into him with unrestrained need.

He felt her body tremble at each impact and her interior muscles start to clamp more tightly around his cock, an indication that she was close.

"Yes, baby!" he encouraged her.

The red tint in her eyes was more pronounced now and behind her parted lips he saw her fangs descend to their full length. Fascinated by the alluring sight, he growled like a beast and lowered his head, tilting it to the side to offer her his neck.

Faye's breath hitched.

The temptation of feeling her fangs in his neck was too strong to resist. He needed her to bite him, to drink from him. When he felt her lips connect with his neck, his heart did a summersault, and his cock jerked in agreement.

"Faye!" he rasped.

Like tiny pinpricks, her fangs drove into his neck, making him shudder. At her first draw on his vein, a bolt of lust shot into his balls.

"Fuck!" was all his lips could utter, before he felt his semen shoot through his cock and explode at the tip.

Then a corresponding shudder coming from Faye's body collided with his spasms as she reached her climax. He continued to press his neck against her lips, not wanting her to stop drinking from him, because every pull on his vein sent another thrilling shiver through his body and into his cock.

For seconds that turned into minutes, Cain continued to thrust his cock into her silken sheath, while Faye's fangs remained lodged in his neck.

17

With a concerned look, Triton peered outside into the dark. The wind was kicking up. Earlier in the day, he'd seen the surf rise. It wasn't a good sign. The storm wasn't far now. In two or three days it would come ashore and whip the city into submission.

Triton shuddered at the thought of the

destruction this would bring to Charleston and other places up and down the coast. The loss of life, the devastation. And there was nothing he could do about it. Without his powers, he was helpless. It wasn't a feeling he was familiar with. If he didn't make progress with Sophia soon, innocent people would have to pay for his mistake. For the first time in his life, he felt true regret about what he'd done. Mortals would have to die, and why? Because Triton couldn't pass up a hot piece of ass and had to anger Zeus.

Somehow he'd have to come clean. What if he explained his situation to Sophia? Would she believe his fantastic story? Would she allow herself to develop feelings for him if she knew what was at stake? Would she give him a fighting chance?

A scream coming from upstairs made him drop the salad bowl to the floor.

Sophia—she was screaming at the top of her lungs. The sound went right through his entire body.

Triton had never moved faster on dry land than when he ran up the stairs now, taking three steps at a time. He stormed into the bedroom and found it empty. Her screams were coming from the bathroom.

Without hesitation he pushed the door handle down, but the door was locked. "Sophia?"

"Triton! Help me!" Her voice sounded terrified.

He stepped back from the door, and a moment later kicked his foot against the lock. Two kicks, and the flimsy door broke open. A wall of hot steam greeted him. He could barely see through the thick foggy soup.

The rattling of the shower door alerted him to Sophia's whereabouts. "I'm here."

Triton rushed to the shower and yanked at the glass door. At first it wouldn't open, but he gave it another forceful pull and it jerked open. He blindly reached into the shower, feeling the hot water assault him.

Sophia's naked body almost fell against him as he pulled her out of the shower. He instinctively pressed her wet form against his body and put his arms around her. She trembled in his embrace.

"I'm here, agapi mou. Everything is fine."

"The water," she sobbed, "it got hotter and hotter."

He let his hands trail over her back in a soothing motion and was surprised that she made no move to get out of his arms. "You should have just turned it off."

"I tried. It didn't work." Another sob tore through her body. "I couldn't switch it off. And then the door was stuck. I couldn't get out." Words poured out of her, and he sensed her fear. "I was trapped." Her panic was evident.

Triton's clothes were already soaked by the water dripping off her delectable curves, but surely any moment now she would realize that she was in his arms, naked and vulnerable. Triton reached for a large bath towel and draped it over her back.

"Let me turn the water off and then we'll get you cleaned up."

Reluctantly, he let go of her and went for the shower. He reached in and felt for the faucets. As he turned them, he noticed how seemingly tight they were. Someone with slippery hands would have difficulty turning them.

When the water finally stopped running, he

turned back to Sophia. She still stood exactly where he'd left her but was now wrapped in the large towel. He took two steps toward her and realized she was still shaking.

"Are you hurt? Did you get burned?" He scanned the parts of her skin that were exposed to his view.

She shook her head.

Without giving it a thought of what she would think, he lifted her into his arms and carried her into the bedroom.

"I couldn't turn it off," she insisted again.

"I know." He sat down on the bed and kept her in his lap, stroking up and down her back all the while. "I'll have someone check out the shower tomorrow and see what's wrong with it."

Her head bobbed up and down in agreement. "I'm not hysterical."

With a hand to her chin, Triton tipped her head up and looked into her tearstained eyes. "I know you're not hysterical."

She sniffed.

"You scared me there for a moment."

Her eyes suddenly changed as if she only now realized that she sat on his lap with only a towel wrapped around her. But he couldn't let her get away now. The fear of thinking that something bad could have happened to her was still pulsing through his body, and he needed to calm himself.

Triton lowered his lips to hers and kissed her. Soft, gentle, without demand. Sophia molded to him. She gave no resistance, only pressed herself closer to him. He'd missed that. He'd missed her. When she sighed, he nudged her lips apart with his tongue and dove into the inviting caverns of her mouth.

A deep moan dislodged from his chest. Damn, but she tasted good. He would skip dinner anytime for a taste of her. Dinner, darn. Never mind, dinner could wait, but he couldn't.

Triton plundered, coaxed, conquered. With every stroke of his tongue against hers, with every lick, the kiss intensified. When he felt her arms come around his neck, the towel dropped off her shoulders. His hands suddenly felt naked skin underneath them. Naked, soft, warm skin.

With a groan he pulled free of the kiss and put a finger on her lips. "Sophia, we have to stop now, or I won't be able to stop at all." Already now, his cock ached for release, pressing against her thigh.

"I'm sorry. I didn't mean to force myself on—"

"Force yourself? Sophia, I'm the one who's taking advantage of the situation," he corrected her. As if she could ever force herself on him. He'd be so lucky!

"Oh." She pulled back a little, giving him a perfect view of her beautiful breasts. His gaze dropped to them, and he was unable to tear himself away from the gorgeous sight.

"Sophia, I, uh." He couldn't think clearly. All his blood was rushing from his brain to his cock, depriving him of his brainpower. Unable to stop himself, his hand reached for her breast. He palmed it gently. "I'm sorry, but I can't stop. I don't know what's happening, but—"

Sophia's soft moan made him lift his gaze. Her lips were parted and still moist from his kiss, and her eyes were closed. "Please don't stop," she whispered and opened her eyes.

"We shouldn't." He couldn't do this, not like that. Before he made love to her, he had to tell her who he was. As least she had to know that they'd met before.

"Sophia, you have to know something," he started, "I have to tell you—"

"Don't you want me anymore?" Disappointment colored her voice, and a tensing of her body told him she was about to bolt.

He tightened his arm around her waist. "I want you." It was all his brain could muster before he sank his mouth back onto her lips and seared them with a passionate kiss. Screw noble, screw the fact he was taking advantage. He wanted her, and her words had told him that she wanted him too. He would tell her everything later.

Triton kneaded her breast. It was the perfect combination of softness and firmness. Her nipple beaded under his caress, and her appreciative moan confirmed that he wasn't misreading her. She was like a soft kitten in his arms, pliable and responsive.

His tongue sought more of her, demanded more intimacy, a deeper penetration. Each stroke sent a bolt akin to one of Zeus's thunderbolts through his groin. He would burst soon if he didn't bury himself in her heat.

His explorations of the delicious caverns of her mouth were met with equal enthusiasm on her part. Her response to him was more than he'd expected. How a mere mortal could ignite his entire body with unbridled lust and desire simply by kissing him, was unfathomable to him. Like little electrical shocks, every contact with her tongue and her lips sent him yet closer to the point of no return.

It was as if Sophia was bent on burning the memory of her kiss into him for eternity, spoiling him for any other woman, for he knew instantly that no other woman had ever kissed him with such abandon, such desire as this mortal did. Surely, no mortal man would be able to resist her after a kiss like this. So, why hadn't she been claimed? Were all mortal men stupid?

Triton took what she offered. And then he took more, coaxed more passion from her body, more desire from her heart. His hands roamed freely over her naked skin now. Forgotten was everything, even the reason why he was with her. Zeus's edict meant nothing in this instant. He didn't want to gain her love merely so he could return home, no, he wanted her love for himself, for his own selfish need. Yes, selfish, because he knew he wasn't the man who'd stay with one woman for eternity. He knew himself too well. But to gain her love would be the sweetest thing.

He moaned deeply when he felt her hand stroke the sensitive skin at his nape. A shiver ran down his spine and settled in his groin. Sophia's touch was as gentle as could be, but the effect was explosive. Triton had never been this sensitive to a woman's touch. He was too familiar with women's hands on his skin to be aroused by a simple touch of fingertips on his neck. But Sophia's fingers turned his entire body into one erogenous zone.

He eased himself back until he felt the mattress support him, keeping Sophia in his arms, then rolled to his side. The towel was now bunched at the foot of the bed and her gloriously naked body wasn't covered by a single stitch. He felt seriously overdressed for the situation.

"Undress me." He wanted her to peel away his clothing at her own pace. The thought excited him.

It was easy enough for her to push his T-shirt up his chest and over his head. Then her hands danced along his skin, caressing his naked chest as if she'd never felt a man's body before. As if she was trying to see him. The moment her hands moved south, he sucked in a sharp breath. His erection strained against his shorts, wanting to be let out.

But Sophia had clearly decided to torture him. Instead of opening the button and sliding down the zipper, she merely cupped his bulge with her palm.

"By the gods!" His voice was strangled. If she continued doing this he'd embarrass himself and come in his pants.

Her lips curved against his mouth. "Are you always this hard?"

She was making jokes? In bed? Was she playing with him? "What are you gonna do about it?"

She squeezed him.

"Besides torturing me," Triton added with a groan.

"If you think that's torture, I have a feeling you're not going to survive this. I've barely started."

He hadn't pegged her to have a wicked streak, but he didn't mind a surprise or two. "You'd better get started, agapi mou, or I'll make a complete idiot out of myself soon." He should be embarrassed about admitting something like that, but for whatever reason, he'd decided to be honest with her.

As he captured her lips again, her hands worked his shorts open and slid them down his hips. He helped her strip him completely before he pulled her body flush to his, his shaft pressing against her stomach.

The scent of her arousal drifted into his nostrils,

and he soaked it up. Turning her so she lay on her back, his hand reached for her thigh and lifted it over his as he slid his own between her parted legs.

When he let go of her lips, she seemed to want to protest, but the moment he trailed kisses along her neck, she sighed. Triton ventured lower, eager to taste her luscious breasts and those hard nipples. Her skin tasted of peaches, its softness enhanced by her recent shower. He glanced at her perfectly round breasts. They were the size of small grapefruits and filled his greedy palms perfectly. He felt the weight in his hand and squeezed, eliciting a soft moan from Sophia. Oh, how he liked a responsive woman.

His tongue darted out and licked over the erect little bud, which couldn't possibly get any harder than it already was. He liked to think that his kisses had aroused her like this, that she only responded to him with such excitement.

Sophia's chest heaved with every breath she took. He stole a glance at her face. Her eyes were closed, her teeth pulling her lower lip into her mouth as if trying to stop herself from screaming.

Triton smiled and sucked her nipple into his mouth. A breathless "Oh" was her response. Never mind that he was aching for release, but showing her the greatest pleasure she could ever have had just become his overriding motive. He wanted her to come apart in his arms. No, not just wanted—needed. Call it male ego or whatever else, but to satisfy this desirable morsel in his arms was more important than anything else at this moment.

With every lap of his tongue against her breasts, her breathing sped up and her body started twisting under his. He took the nipple in his mouth, tugging on it slightly. Encouraged by her moans, he gave it a tentative bite. She nearly arched off the bed, thrusting her breast farther into his mouth. So he repeated the same on her other breast, before he released those beautiful round globes and moved down to her stomach.

Her belly wasn't completely flat but had just enough flesh to provide a soft cushion for a man—or a god. Triton planted a kiss on her navel and headed for the ultimate prize. The scent of her arousal beckoned, and he couldn't deny the draw any longer. If he didn't taste her now, he'd die of starvation.

With his hands on her thighs he nudged them apart and made a space for himself between them.

"Look at me," he ordered her. Sophia's eyes flew open. How he would have liked for her to really see him now, to see the desire in his eyes, but Sophia's gaze didn't lock with his, even though she looked in his direction. Nevertheless, Triton wanted her to acknowledge what he was about to do. "Sophia, I'll feast on you until you come in my mouth."

A gasp was her only response. It was all he needed.

He was fully aware of the intimacy of his actions. And he wanted this intimacy with her, wanted to learn every inch of her body so he would never forget what she felt like. Always remember her taste.

Triton dropped his gaze back to the dark triangle of curls sitting at the apex of her thighs. Just below, her pink flesh glistened with moisture. She was weeping for him, yearning for his touch.

Slowly, savoring every second, he dropped his head to her pussy and pressed a soft kiss into her curls. Then he nudged down, bringing his mouth to her nether lips. When he took his first lick and tasted her honey, his body went rigid. He wouldn't last long—no, this delectable taste would send him over the edge in no time.

Sophia writhed against him, asking for more, and he was all too willing to give her more. His tongue lapped at her moist folds with the eagerness of a young man who'd only just discovered the carnal arts, yet Triton was an experienced man—simply tasting her quivering pussy shouldn't send him into the tailspin he was currently finding himself in. His desire for her spiraled, taking over his body and mind, robbing him of any control he'd ever had in her presence.

Whatever she wanted, he'd give it to her. No demand would be too great or too outlandish to fulfill if only it meant she would continue to allow him to taste her body. He would forego ambrosia and even wine for the rest of his immortal life, if only he could drink from her instead.

Triton tried to ignore the bolts of pleasure charging through his body and igniting his cock, but to no avail. What she did to him was too powerful to ignore even for a second. His body was on fire, and no swim in the cold depths of the ocean could douse those flames and cool the fire.

He licked upwards to the base of her curls, finding her engorged clit. His lips settled around it, pulling it into his mouth. Sophia panted heavily and twisted under his hold.

"You're not going anywhere," he whispered against her skin.

"Oh God."

Yes, he was her god tonight, and he'd make her

come. Triton sucked on the little bud and licked his tongue over it in a rhythm Sophia's body set for him. He released one of her thighs and trailed his finger to her wet pussy. Not letting go of her clit, he drove his middle finger into her tight sheath. Her muscles convulsed around him instantly.

His own control shattered.

A second later, he felt her tremble as she climaxed. He didn't release her clit. Instead, he kept his lips firmly lodged around it, and every so often he flicked his tongue over it, prolonging her orgasm until she finally stilled under him.

He pulled himself up to her and wrapped her into his arms. She molded to him instantly. When her hand moved to his cock, he took her wrist and stopped her. "I'm afraid, I came the moment you did."

Like a green kid he'd shot his seed into the sheets. He should feel embarrassed, but instead he felt strangely content.

"Told you, you wouldn't survive it." She smirked.

Triton laughed. When was the last time he'd laughed in bed? He couldn't remember. "Give me a few minutes and I'll get back at you for that."

Without waiting for a reply, he took her lips and kissed her, giving her a preview of what she'd have to expect when he finally made love to her for real, when he finally thrust into her with all his might and made her surrender to him.

Evidently, her stomach had other ideas as it growled loudly, making him interrupt his kiss. "Hungry?"

"Mmm hmm."

"Okay then, let me make us some dinner."

155

18

Isabella waited for Raphael to retrieve their cloaks and accepted another couple's well-wishes. After a few dances with her new husband, during which he'd plied her ears with scandalous words not suitable to be repeated anywhere, he'd finally declared that they'd spent sufficient time at the ball and could return home.

She was relieved. Despite the fact that the Doge had declared their marriage legitimate, she didn't like the stares people gave her. Was it her gown, or was it her husband they looked at? Or maybe it was the fact that she felt flushed, not by the warmth in the large hall, but by the words Raphael had whispered to her on a continuous basis. And by his hard length, which she'd felt while dancing with him.

She shivered when she felt Raphael's hands on her shoulders, spreading her cloak over her, then tying it at her throat.

"You were the most beautiful woman at the ball." His breath caressed her neck, and she tilted it slightly, offering it to him. He pressed a soft kiss against her skin, and she felt her blood warm. A moment later, he turned her to face him.

"Here, put this on."

She looked down at his hands and took a mask from him. "Why do you want me to wear a mask?"

"I'll explain later."

He put his own half-mask on and helped her tie hers. It hid most of her face, but her mouth remained free and unimpeded. When she turned and looked into the full-length mirror in the hallway, all she saw was a stranger in a long red dress covered by a black cloak. The black mask made her face unrecognizable.

"Come," Raphael urged her and led her into the night.

The streets were teeming with revelers, many wearing masks, some elaborate, others as simple as her own. Everybody was the same. Class was forgotten. It was how it was meant to be. During carnival, a pauper could be a prince. A noble could be a pirate. A whore could be a lady.

Isabella looked with wonder at the different people and masks as Raphael led her through the busy alleys around Piazza San Marco. The further they walked, the quieter the streets became. She barely noticed how far they'd gone because she was so fascinated with the activities in the streets.

She was surprised when Raphael suddenly stopped under an arched walkway and pressed her back to a wall behind her, his body flush against hers. "And now, my sweet wife, it's time to consummate our marriage. I think I've waited long enough." The predatory glint in his eyes was unmistakable.

Isabella gasped in shock. "Here?"

His lips ghosted over her skin, his breath caressing her as he answered.

"Yes, my beautiful angel, right here. That's why we're wearing masks. I'll ravish you here, where any passerby might see us. Yet, they won't know who we are. All they'll think is that a man is fucking a whore, and they won't care. Maybe they'll simply watch."

She tried to push him away, and with him her own scandalous desire to do just what he was suggesting. Her body already responded to his salacious words, her sex clenching in anticipation of his body claiming her. And the thought that somebody could see them sent a hot flame through her core. No, she couldn't allow this to happen.

Raphael encircled her wrists and held them to the wall, then dipped his head to where her bosom heaved. He licked his tongue over her twin swells in a low and sensual stroke and inhaled.

"I can smell your arousal, my love."

Panic gripped her. If she allowed him to do this,

he would realize that she was no lady, that she was no better than a whore, because only a whore would allow herself to be ravished in such a public place. And then? Would he toss her away when he saw what she really was? A deeply disturbed woman with lusty feelings, more debauched than any whore in the city?

"Please, Raphael, let us go home," she pleaded, but knew her voice was hoarse with the lust she could barely contain. She didn't understand why he conjured these feelings up in her. Her first husband never had. She'd been the dutiful wife, and while she had enjoyed when Giovanni had bedded her, she'd never lost control or felt the desire to do scandalous things like those Raphael proposed.

Isabella felt her bodice loosening and realized that Raphael was undoing some of the hooks that held her dress up. She tried to protest, but couldn't because his lips on her skin made her brain unable to form any words. When his hands pulled down her bodice by only a few centimeters, it was sufficient for her breasts to pop out of their cage. Cold air blasted against them, tightening her nipples instantly.

Greedily, Raphael clamped his mouth over one nipple and sucked, while his hand cupped her other breast and kneaded it. Isabella couldn't stop the moan from leaving her lips, just as she couldn't stop the liquid that pooled between her legs.

"Oh, God," she whispered breathlessly.

Her nipple popped out of his mouth, and he used his fingers to pull on it. Then he looked at her, his eyes clouded with the same passion she'd seen in him the night before. "Open my breeches and take my cock out."

Without thinking, she followed his order while he

sank his lips onto her other nipple. With shaking fingers, she reached for his flap and started unbuttoning it. Her hand grazed his hard length. His moan was so deep and loud, she heard it echo in the archway. But by now she didn't care who would see or hear them. She wanted him, wanted his hard shaft to drive into her and claim her.

When his trousers were finally open, she wrapped her palm around him and squeezed the velvety skin covering his marble-hard manhood. She loved the feel of it, soft on hard. Two opposites, yet one incomplete without the other. So perfect and beautiful.

She felt Raphael's hands on her shoulders, pushing her down. "Suck me," he ordered.

Isabella dropped to her knees in front of him and found his shaft pointing right at her mouth.

"Yes, suck me like a whore. Because tonight, my dear wife, you're my whore, and you'll do whatever I want."

The words should have shocked her, but all she thought of was to put her lips onto his flesh and make him beg for release. She didn't feel degraded because he'd called her a whore. Instead, she felt powerful, because by being on her knees she would bring him to his. She licked her lips and took her first taste of his flesh.

~ ~ ~

Raphael's control nearly shattered when Isabella's lips closed around his cock and slid down on him. White hot heat surrounded him, nearly paralyzing him. He braced himself against the wall behind her, trying to steady his shaking legs. She would be his undoing.

Never had a woman's mouth given him such

instant, overwhelming pleasure. "Fuck," he let out, his brain unable to form any other word since it had turned to the consistency of molasses. He tried to steel himself against the onslaught of sensations she unleashed on him, but to no avail.

Like a barrage of cannonballs, they plowed into him: burning him, searing him, branding him. Yes, she was branding him with her mouth, with the laps of her tongue against his hard flesh, with her breath that whispered against his length, the hands that stroked him in concert with her mouth. She was spoiling him for any other woman, making certain he would never want to be touched by anybody else, never feel another woman's mouth on him but hers.

Like a witch, she spun her spells around him, her cheeks hollowing as she sucked on him harder, her fingernails scraping against his tight sac where his balls burned like hellfire, the pressure mounting as in a volcano. God, she would suck the life out of him if she could. And at this point he wasn't so sure it was beyond her capabilities.

Another lick against his mushroomed head and he pulled himself out of her mouth, hissing sharply. He couldn't take any more.

"I wasn't done," Isabella complained.

Without a word, Raphael grabbed her and lowered her onto the stone bench he'd seen in the corner, high enough so he could remain standing when he fucked her. Then he tossed up her skirts and reached for her drawers. With one swoop, he ripped them into shreds, ignoring her surprised look. He had no more patience than a sailor who'd spent the last months at sea.

Her arousal engulfed him. "Now I'll fuck you, my

beautiful whore! I'll fuck you until you scream." And with one single thrust he seated himself in her drenched pussy. She convulsed around him, making him still instantly. "Oh, yes, you love being ravished out here, don't you?" When she didn't say anything, he ordered, "Answer me!"

Isabella's breathless "Yes" was more of a moan than a word. It suited him just fine. And strangely enough, it helped him gain his control back. No, this delectable, passionate woman would not gain the upper hand.

Slowly, Raphael pulled his cock from her silken heat, only to let it slide over her little pearl. She twisted underneath him, but he held her hips in a vice grip so she couldn't escape his torture. He would make her confront her desires. Now. Here. He would break down her defenses and free the passionate woman inside her.

Not giving her any indication of what he was about to do, he plunged his hard length back into her, making her release a startled cry. "Oh, yes, never think you're safe from my cock. Because I'll take your wet cunt with it whenever and wherever I want." He deliberately used crude words to shock her, all the while sliding back and forth in her tight sheath, her honey so slick, he felt like drowning all over again. Only this time, it was a pleasurable kind of drowning.

When he heard a sound behind him, he twisted his head. "It appears we have company." He briefly glanced at the well-dressed gentleman, who'd entered the covered archway and was looking at them.

Raphael felt Isabella's instant reaction and recognized it as her flight instinct. But he wouldn't allow her to follow it. Instead, he continued to pump into her sweet depths and reached for her ample breasts, which bobbed with each of his thrusts.

"When you're done with her, I'll take her," the man behind him offered.

Raphael growled. "I won't be done with her for a long time." A very long time. "She's mine for the night. I bought this whore, and I'm going to make certain I'll get my money's worth." He grinned at Isabella when he noticed her shocked face. "So, no, you can't fuck her, unless, of course, she consents."

Isabella's protest was instantaneous. "No!"

Raphael chuckled.

"As you can see, she only wants my cock. But if you care to watch, step closer for a better view." He didn't care whether the man watched or not, but he would never allow him to lay one single finger on her. Isabella would not be shared with anybody. But while her mask provided her anonymity, and him as well, he would drive her lust higher by the knowledge that they were being watched.

The man's footsteps confirmed that he'd accepted his offer. Raphael could see how he stood only a short distance from them to the side, so he could see both Isabella's naked breasts as well as her cunt and how Raphael's cock plunged in and out of her.

"She has a beautiful cunt, this whore, don't you think?" he asked the stranger as he sliced back into her heat, kneading her breasts in his palms.

But the man didn't answer. From the corner of his eye, Raphael could see why: the man's hand had freed his own cock. Hard and thick, it strutted from his breeches as he now pumped it in his right hand.

"I see you agree," he commented and brought his attention back to Isabella, who'd followed his glance.

Her mouth dropped open.

"Yes, he's stroking himself, wishing it was your hot cunt he's pumping into. Does that excite you?" He delivered a hard thrust, and she snapped her gaze back to him, dropping her lids as if in shame. With another thrust, he jolted her. "Oh, no, you won't turn away. I want you to watch him watch you as I fuck you." Her eyes went wide behind her mask. He knew she wanted to watch, but was too ashamed to admit it.

He pinched her nipples hard until she cried out, her lips quivering, her breath at a fever pitch.

"Now watch him. But remember, it is my cock that's inside you. My cock that fills you."

He wanted to possess her, every cell of her. And he wanted the whole world to know she was his, his to drive to ecstasy, his to pleasure. His body set his rhythm now, plunging deep and hard into her with long strokes.

He noticed her pull her lips between her teeth as she watched the other man stroke his own cock. Raphael heard the grunts the man let out, but he only saw her, his beautiful angel, ecstasy written all over her body.

He released one of her tits and dropped his hand to her pearl. She snapped her head back to him as he rubbed his thumb over it. A moment later, she cried out, and her muscles clamped around his cock, igniting his own climax.

His seed shot from his balls through the length of his cock and exploded from its tip, pumping into her channel, flooding her with it.

But he barely noticed any of it as his entire body was gripped by his orgasm, shaking him to the core.

Nothing had ever felt as raw and earth-shattering as the consummation of his marriage.

19

Maya felt his warm hand and looked up to meet his gaze. "Once you're normal again, you'll want somebody else, not me."

"Didn't you hear what I said to you earlier? That I love you."

The words felt good, but still she couldn't believe

them. "Yes, you said that, but you also said you want a child. Once you realize that you could have anybody when your deformity is gone, then why wouldn't you want to be with somebody who can give you children?"

Before she knew what was happening, Gabriel pulled her into his arms. "I don't care about that," he said gruffly. "All I ever wanted out of life is a wife who loves me and accepts me for what I am. Becoming a father would have been a bonus, but I don't care about that, not enough. Do you really think I would give up this chance at happiness merely because we won't be able to have children?"

"You mean that?" Her heart beat into her throat.

"I mean it. But—"

So there was a but. She shouldn't have rejoiced too early. Her shoulders dropped in defeat.

"You have to accept me, and once I tell you what the witch found out, it's up to you to make a decision. I love you. I want you to know that, but I can't ask you to be mine until you know what I am. It wouldn't be fair."

Now confusion set in. There was a hesitation in his voice she hadn't heard before, almost as if he was uncertain of how to broach the subject. "What you are? What do you mean?"

"I'm not a full-blooded vampire."

The news didn't mean anything to her. How could he not be a full-blooded vampire? By everything she'd seen so far, he was definitely a vampire, and a very potent one at that. She'd seen his fangs, felt his strength. She'd seen him drink blood. "How can you not be a vampire?"

"I am, but I'm not, at least not fully. I wasn't

human when I was turned. I just never realized that until now. My turning was much like yours, and now I understand why. Like you I almost died a second time, as if my body was rejecting becoming a vampire. But I pulled through, just like you did."

She remembered all too well how painful it had been. "I live because of you."

He pressed his forehead against hers. "But I don't ever want you to think you owe me for that. I did it for a very selfish reason: I wanted you to live, because I wanted you to be mine. Right there, that moment when I first saw you lying on that bed in Samson's house, I knew I would love you."

"How could you know that? You didn't know anything about me." Yet, there was such certainty in his words.

"My body recognized you. We're alike, Maya, much more than I could have ever guessed. I'm part satyr, and so are you."

The news hit her like a freight train slamming into a brick wall. Satyr? "A beast with hooves?"

Gabriel shook his head. "You mean a Minotaur. Satyrs are different. They are mythical creatures, part man, part animal, but the animal part only manifests itself in their strength and thirst for carnal pleasures and in the male of the species in one other piece of anatomy. Otherwise our bodies look entirely human. All that about hooves and horns came later in mythology. Anyway, that's why I never knew. I didn't know my father, so there was nobody to explain to me what I was."

"And you say I'm a satyr too. But how?" It didn't make any sense. She'd always felt human.

"You're aware that you were adopted?"

She was surprised he knew. "Of course. My parents never made a secret of it. Besides, they're blond and fair skinned, and I'm anything but."

"Your biological parents, or at least your father, must have been a satyr."

"How can the witch be so certain? She hasn't done any tests on me." The witch's claim was too outlandish to believe.

"She doesn't have to because of what's happened to me. I've gone through a change." He swallowed hard. Maya could see his Adam's Apple undulate.

"What kind of change?"

"After we had sex."

"Damn it, Gabriel, would you just come out with it." She planted her hands at her waist, but instead of releasing her, he only pulled her closer.

"This change." He pressed his hips into hers. "The mass of flesh you saw. It's changed. It only does that after a satyr has sex with his satyr mate for the first time. Maya, it's turned into a second penis because you and I had sex."

She gasped, sucking the air into her lungs quickly to supply her brain with oxygen. He had two penises? She pulled away from him and instantly noticed his disappointed frown. But she couldn't concern herself with that right now. Her hand went to the place where his jeans bulged. When her palm connected with the hardness beneath, he jerked for a moment before he pressed against it.

Then she felt it. There wasn't just the outline of one erect cock pulsing under her palm, but she could clearly feel a second one, just as hard but a fraction smaller. It strained against the confinement of his pants.

"I want to see." She licked her lips and went for the zipper.

His hand stopped her, locking her in place. "Maya." His voice was strained, and when she looked at him, she saw the barely contained desire in his eyes. He looked like he wanted to devour her, and considering what she felt under her hand, she had a pretty good idea what he wanted to devour her with.

Her heartbeat kicked up as her body responded in kind. There was nothing that she wanted more than to get her hands on his twin cocks and touch them, take them into her mouth one by one and suck them until he begged her to stop.

"This is not a science lesson."

Was that what he thought she wanted to do, merely examine him? "If you don't get those pants off right now and make love to me, I swear, the moment the sun sets, I'll walk out of here and you'll never see me again."

His droll look was priceless. "You want me to make love to you, and you actually think I would turn you down? Maya, I'm a vampire, I'm a satyr, but above all—I'm a man."

~ ~ ~

Gabriel's brain did a somersault. Maya accepted him for what he was. A small confident smile curled around her red lips, and the glint in her eyes was the same as he'd seen in her before, back in the living room where they'd made love like crazy. "You want me?"

"Yes, and given that we can't get out of here— until sunset anyway—I can't think of anything better than having sex, can you?" she asked and gave him a coquettish wink.

Neither could he. Gabriel folded her into his embrace, his mouth hovering over hers. She lifted her head and offered her lips to him. "Kiss me."

He gave a little smile. "I love kissing you." Then he fitted his lips to hers and pressed a soft kiss to her mouth. A low sigh was Maya's response. Her breath bounced against his, and he parted his lips to drink her in. His senses flooded with her scent and taste.

Gabriel let his hands roam over her back. One drifted down to her ass, cupping her with his large palm and pressing her closer into his hips. He felt his twin erections press into the soft flesh of her stomach, while her full breasts flattened against the hard planes of his chest. Everything felt so right. She was the perfect woman, the yin to his yang.

He speared his tongue and dove into her, dueled with her, stroked, nibbled, and sucked. Her soft moans were music to his ears, her hands on him encouragement to continue with what he was doing. Already Maya had pulled his shirt from his pants and was now sliding her hands onto his naked chest, making him hiss in a much needed breath.

"Now show me what you've got," she whispered against his lips, breathing as heavily as he did.

"Impatient?" He kissed the side of her mouth.

"Curious."

"Scared?" His lips trailed to her neck where he felt her vein throb under his lips.

"Eager," she pressed out between soft moans.

"I hoped that this time I could have offered you a soft bed." The first time he'd taken her against the wall in the living room, and now? He would have liked to make this more special for her.

"I don't care."

"It won't be very comfortable for you."

She pulled his head to hers and looked at him. "I don't want comfortable. I want you."

He lost himself in her dark eyes. "And I want you. But this time, you will come with me if it's the last thing I do."

"Male pride?"

It had nothing to do with pride. "Survival instinct."

She raised an eyebrow, not understanding, so he explained, "I won't have you leave me because I can't satisfy you."

Her lips curled up, and she pressed her hips provocatively against his groin. "You might just have what I need."

"Hold that thought." He pulled himself out of her embrace and walked to the supply cupboard.

"What are you doing?"

Gabriel opened the cupboard and examined the contents. "Making us more comfortable. I can't get you a proper bed, but at least I can provide some of this." He pulled out a couple of thick blankets, which had been shrink-wrapped to protect them from dust and moisture. He ripped the plastic open and pulled them out of their protective covers.

With a few steps he was at the corner where several cots were stacked up. He pulled one aside and spread the blankets onto it to provide more cushioning.

"You're a very practical man," Maya commented.

Gabriel turned to her and smiled. "You'll find out over time that I have many other useful qualities."

She hummed. "Mmm, hmm. Two in particular." Her eyes dropped to his crotch. Heat instantly shot through his body. She was direct, and he appreciated that in her. There was no beating around the bush about what she wanted. And what Maya clearly wanted right now, was him—or rather his two very erect and eager cocks. And he wasn't going to deprive her of that pleasure, or him for that matter. Even if he was a little apprehensive about his own desires right now—his own very dark and very forbidden desires. Because surely a woman like her would never agree to—

"Have you changed your mind?" she asked and stepped closer, her enticing scent instantly drugging him.

"Not a chance." Gabriel reached for her hand and pulled her toward him. "May I undress you?" For some reason, he felt nervous. This was a big step. If she didn't like what he was about to do, she could still leave him. And he wouldn't let that happen. No, he'd keep his own dark desire hidden so he wouldn't frighten her away. Even though he knew exactly what he wanted. The thought of taking Maya from behind with both cocks thrusting into her, one in her sweet pussy, the other in the dark and forbidden passage he suddenly craved, made his erections throb uncontrollably.

"If I can undress you at the same time," she answered then, interrupting his debauched thoughts.

His hands went to her T-shirt, and slowly he pulled it out of her jeans. When he tugged on it, she lifted her hands over her head and allowed him to free her from it. She wore no bra.

~ ~ ~

Maya felt a whoosh of cold air against her naked breasts and sensed her nipples tighten. Yet she knew it wasn't the cold air that excited her, it was the way Gabriel looked at her: with barely leashed desire. He was hungry for her, just as hungry as she was for him. The things he'd told her about him and about herself suddenly all made sense.

Her unexplainable fevers, her insatiable need for sex, and her inability to feel satisfied with the men she'd been with. Would that all be different now? Would Gabriel satisfy her?

Maya reached for the buttons of his shirt and eased them open one-by-one, exposing his muscular chest. As soon as she stripped him of it, she went for his jeans. Beneath the denim, the bulge had grown to massive proportions.

Two cocks. She knew instinctively what that meant. What was supposed to happen. He would take her with both of them. The desires she'd never been able to put into words and express finally lay within her grasp. She knew what her body had always craved, yet at the same time her brain had tried to push away. To feel two cocks in her at the same time. Here was Gabriel, part vampire, part satyr, who could give her what she'd never dared to dream about: the sexual satisfaction she'd always craved, the dark desires she'd never allowed herself to voice.

When she eased the top button of his jeans open and slid the zipper down, Gabriel exhaled sharply. With both hands she pushed his pants over his hips, then down his legs where he quickly chucked his boots and stepped out of his jeans.

Maya's gaze went back to his boxers, which tented in the front. She slid her hands between skin and waistband and pushed the fabric down, finally exposing what she'd wanted for so long. She barely noticed as he freed himself of the boxer shorts and his socks, so fascinated was she by the sight in front of her.

Even when he helped her get out of her own pants and shoes, she could not take her eyes off the sight.

"Gabriel, you're beautiful," she whispered, her hands reaching for his cocks. Each of her hands grasped one erect shaft, feeling the smooth skin and the hardness beneath. Their purple heads pumped full with blood, primed to explode, pointed at her, fairly asking for attention.

"Fuck!" he gasped breathlessly. "Baby, you're robbing me of my control."

She let a wicked smile curve around her lips as she looked up in his face. "Isn't that the point?"

"No, the point is for me to satisfy you first."

Before she could react, he picked her up in his arms and carried her to the makeshift bed. He gently lowered her onto it. She stretched her naked body out, appreciating the softness the two blankets underneath her provided.

With one leg braced on the floor, Gabriel lowered his body, one knee wedged between her legs. He began kissing her neck. His lips trailed along the sensitive skin just below her earlobe, then farther down, hovering over her pulse where her neck met her shoulder. He suckled at the spot.

Then his lips traveled south, reaching her breasts and the hard nipples that topped them. He palmed one globe and sucked the tip into his mouth, his moan telling her how much he enjoyed the action. Her body heated under his caress, her core turning to liquid and pooling at the apex of her thighs.

Maya shifted, opening her legs wider to allow his hard shafts to rub against her as she wiggled.

"Getting impatient?" he whispered as he licked leisurely over her breast.

"I want you inside me."

"I'm not done here," he claimed and continued torturing her breasts in the most delicious way she'd ever been tortured by a man. His hands kneaded one peak while his mouth suckled on the other almost greedily as if he couldn't get enough of her.

"You can have more of that later," she coaxed him, "but right now, just give me what I want."

He glanced up at her, and his eyes blinked in agreement. "Only because you're asking so nicely," he joked.

Gabriel shifted his body, and suddenly his lower cock nudged at the entrance to her moist channel, while his upper cock was poised at her curly triangle. With his finger he touched her folds. "So wet, baby." Then he dipped into her wetness and spread the moisture over her clit, eliciting a strangled moan from her throat.

But before she could press against his finger, he'd withdrawn his hand. Instead, he guided his upper cock to her clit and rubbed over the now moist button. "Now I'm ready." His voice was a rough rumble coming deep from within his chest.

The moment he thrust forward, his cock drove deep into her, while the second one slid over her clit, stroking her with perfect pressure. He filled her, stretching her so she could accommodate his size. He felt larger than he'd felt that time in the living room, but maybe it was just the position she found herself in: imprisoned underneath his large body, his thighs rubbing against her, his cocks thrusting in concert with each other.

She'd never felt anything this perfect. With wonder, she felt her body join his in perfect synchrony. Her breathless moans mingled with his, their bodies writhing against each other, dancing on a cloud of weightlessness. She felt like falling, yet knew she was safe in his arms, safe underneath his strong body as his thrusts intensified and his rhythm became faster.

With every stroke and every slide, her core heated, her heartbeat raced in a frantic beat toward the inevitable. Gabriel never once broke eye contact, but kept his gaze locked with hers as if to assure her that he could read what she wanted, what she needed from him. His skin glistened with sweat, and his hand came up to stroke her face. "Maya, baby." It looked as if he wanted so say more, but didn't.

Maya felt her clit swell farther with every slide of his cock over it. She sensed the start of her climax in the soles of her feet. And as the ripples traveled upwards, her breath came in shallow pants. She caught Gabriel's smile a moment before the waves of her orgasm hit her. Of its own volition, a scream left her throat. She'd never before screamed during sex. And she'd never come with a man's cock inside her. "Oh, God."

On the last wave of her climax, she felt him stiffen, and a moment later his cock pulsed violently inside her, shooting his seed into her. At the same time, she felt a wetness on her stomach and registered that his second cock had exploded at the same time.

"Oh, God, baby!" he ground out, his eyes mirroring the disbelief in his voice. Even as he collapsed on top of her, he braced himself so she wouldn't carry his entire weight.

He leaned his forehead to hers and breathed heavily. "I had no idea. Maya, I've never come like that. Never so intensely."

She smiled and pressed a soft kiss on his lips. "Neither have I."

Gabriel kissed her deeply, his tongue sweeping against hers in long and commanding strokes. When he released her lips, his mouth trailed down to her neck again, suckling at the same spot where he'd suckled before. But this time, his teeth gently grazed against her skin. Out of nowhere a vision entered her mind: of him sinking his fangs into her and drinking her blood.

She gasped and felt him pull back. "Did I hurt you?"

Maya looked into his passion-clouded eyes and swallowed hard. And before she could stop herself, she expressed her deepest wish. "Bite me."

~ ~ ~

Gabriel groaned. She wanted him to bite her? She was dangling his greatest temptation in front of him when he had no right to take this much from her. Not with what was going on inside him right now, not with the urge that had started boiling up in him, the urge to do unspeakable things to her. Things no decent woman would allow a man to do, things even most whores would refuse.

"Oh Maya, you have no idea what you're offering me." Conflicting emotions warred in his mind: desire on one hand, caution on the other. He couldn't bind her to him when she might be running from him, recoiling from him when she found out what he

178

wanted from her. To fuck her in the most bestial way. She couldn't possibly want that.

"What's wrong?"

"If I bite you while we have sex and you take my blood at the same time, we would create a blood-bond—Maya, a blood-bond is forever. There's no way out."

Her response came faster than he'd expected. "You don't want forever?"

He recognized the disappointment in her eyes, the hurt. He couldn't let her believe that, not even for a second. "I want forever, but there's something you have to know about me first." He paused and closed his eyes before he spoke again. Laying himself bare was the hardest thing he'd ever done, but she deserved it, deserved honesty about the darkness inside him.

"I want to take you in the most bestial way you can imagine, and I don't think I could suppress that kind of lust for long. Now that I know what I am, now that I realize what my body wants, I can't hold it back much longer." He opened his eyes. "Maya, I want to claim you with both my cocks at the same time, take your pussy with one and your—" He broke off and looked away, not wanting to see the disgust that would soon flood her eyes. "And your ass with the other. Don't you see? It's depraved. I shouldn't want something like that, but I do. If you bond with me, you won't escape that, you'd have to endure it."

His heart beat frantically in his chest. What if she walked away from him now?

"Endure?" With her hand to his chin, she forced him to look at her. "Gabriel, I want everything you have to offer. We're both satyrs. What makes you think that I don't have the exact same wish? What makes you think that I don't crave being taken like that?"

His eyes widened in surprise. "You want this?" He searched her eyes and couldn't see anything that looked even remotely like disgust.

"Why else would a satyr have two cocks but to use them to satisfy his mate?"

First, she'd called him perfect, and now Maya offered to fulfill his darkest desire. In that moment, Gabriel knew he was the luckiest man alive. She was the personification of everything he'd ever wished for: a home, a loving wife, a fulfilled sex life. And while life would be even more perfect if they could have children, it wasn't important enough for him to give her up. His mind was made up—in fact it always had been.

"I pledge my heart and my life to you." His voice almost cracked as he continued, "I want a blood-bond with you, but not here. I want you to have a memory you'll always look back on as special." He looked around the room to indicate that this wasn't it. "When we bond, it will be in a room full of red candles. We'll lie on crisp white sheets as we make love, and everything will be perfect. I promise you."

She smiled at him. "Could it be that you're a hopeless romantic?"

"Not hopeless—hope*ful*." He brushed his lips to hers. "Just promise me you won't tell anybody. Otherwise it might undermine my position."

She rolled her eyes. "Men!" And then she laughed. The sound went right through him and warmed his heart. Maya looked happy, and he promised himself that he'd do everything in his power to make sure she was always this happy.

She seemed to realize that he was staring at her, and her laugh subsided. Her eyes locked with his, and he felt as if she looked into his soul. "I love you."

He choked back the tears that threatened to unman him at her unexpected declaration. "My heart is yours."

The kiss that followed turned from sweet and gentle to heated and demanding in the blink of an eye. He was still inside her and growing hard again, having remained semi-hard the entire time they had talked.

He eased himself out of her hot sheath and broke the kiss.

"Something wrong?" she asked, her voice soft, almost sleepy. He recognized it as that of a very satisfied woman. And it satisfied him to know that he'd been able to make her come.

"Nothing's wrong, baby. I want to make love to you the satyr way, but I don't want to hurt you."

He lifted himself off the cot and marched to the supply cabinet. Earlier, he'd seen medical supplies in there, and if he wasn't mistaken there was a jar of Vaseline among them. It would have to do. When he turned back to her, the lubricant in his hands, Maya had turned onto her stomach. Gabriel sucked in a breath. She would be his undoing, for how would he ever make it out of bed in the next few hundred years with her by his side as his mate?

He let his gaze travel over the curve of her back, then over the soft swells of her round ass, before he followed her shapely legs. She had parted them slightly, allowing him to see the dark curls at their apex, curls that glistened with moisture. Her pink nether lips oozed with the seed he'd planted in her, and he felt the urge to slide his cock back into her enticing channel so it would remain inside her. It was a silly thought because he knew his seed wouldn't take hold in her. Even though—hadn't the witch said something about satyr females being fertile? But there had been so much to take in that he wasn't sure he'd heard right.

Without haste, he approached the cot and sat down at its edge. He wasn't done admiring her beauty and counting his blessings. Despite the scar on his face, despite his two cocks and the dark desires they represented, he'd been graced with the most amazing gift of his life: a woman who wanted him despite everything.

"You're beautiful," he whispered and stroked his palm down the length of her naked back. "I wish I were a painter. I would paint you just like this."

She turned her head to him and smiled. "I'd much rather you made love to me than paint me." Then her eyes zeroed in on the jar in his hands. "Touch me."

Gabriel inhaled deeply and dipped his finger into the lubricant. "I promise I'll be as gentle as possible."

Maya closed her eyes and sighed. When he slid his hand along her crack, her ass arched toward him, opening herself up to him. Helped by the lubrication, his finger ran smoothly down the incline until he reached the tight ring of muscle that guarded the entrance to her dark portal. He heard her suck in a breath when his finger lingered there. Slowly he circled the bud, spreading the lubricant.

The thought of breaching the gate to this dark cave made his body pump more blood into his cocks. He looked down at himself, where his twin shafts stood erect, eager to impale her. Ahead were previously unknown pleasures, and he felt nervousness creep into his skin. He didn't want to hurt her. "I've never done this before."

"Neither have I," she confessed.

With barely noticeable pressure, he probed her dark hole and felt her ease toward him. The tip of his finger slipped past the tight muscle, gripping his digit tightly.

A low moan came from Maya, and he could only echo it. Never in his life had he felt anything this tight. Maya's pussy had gripped him like a snug glove, but the knowledge that she would soon squeeze him even tighter left him breathless. He wouldn't last. His cock wouldn't survive this delight for longer than ten seconds. And maybe it was good that way—he wouldn't subject her to this ordeal for too long. He still didn't believe that she really wanted this as much as he did. More likely she allowed him this dark treat because she wanted him and wouldn't deny him.

He drove his finger deeper into her, giving her time to adjust to the invasion.

"More," she whispered, her voice clouded with passion, hoarse. Her encouragement eradicated his worry that she was hurting, and he slid deeper until his finger was lodged inside her as far as it would go. Then slowly he eased back out, took another dollop of lubrication and pressed back in.

Now Maya was panting heavily, her hips flexing, forcing him inside her faster than before. "Yes!"

Her enthusiasm wasn't lost on him. Did she actually like this? His heart swelled as she fell into a rhythm, alternately pushing her ass back, then pulling forward, so his finger would thrust back and forth inside her. When he recognized that she wanted more, he took charge and finger-fucked her pretty ass the way she demanded it: with long, deep strokes that increased in speed as her breathing became short and shallow.

When she demanded more, he eased a second finger into her, stretching her wider. He couldn't tear himself away from the erotic sight. As his fingers disappeared inside her dark portal, his own heart reached a fever pitch, his cocks oozed pre-cum in anticipation, and his entire body tingled pleasantly.

But he couldn't wait any longer. He shifted and knelt behind her, between her spread thighs. "Get on your hands and knees," he coaxed her and slipped his fingers out of her before he pulled her ass into his groin.

Gabriel once again helped himself to the lubricant and spread it over his upper cock, before he placed it at her entrance. His lower cock was already poised at her pussy, ready to enter her. Her honey teased the head of his hard shaft, promising him pleasure beyond his wildest imagination.

With one hand he held onto her hip, he used the other to guide his second cock as he pressed forward. Almost without effort his tip disappeared inside her, pushing past the tight ring.

"Oh God," she panted.

"Too much?" He was ready to pull out if he caused her pain.

She merely shook her head and eased back toward him, taking him deeper. His lower cock slipped inside her pussy without resistance while his upper one pressed forward. Inside her, he could feel both his cocks rub against the thin membrane between her two channels.

"Oh, fuck!" He couldn't stop himself from cursing at the intense pleasure that spread in his body. Before he knew what he was doing, he thrust forward, seating himself in her to the hilts. The way her body gripped him, squeezed him, he almost lost control right there. "Ohfuckohfuckohfuck…" Nothing had ever felt this perfect in his long life. No other pleasure had ever been this intense. If he died right now, he'd die a happy man.

When Maya wiggled beneath him, obviously to entice him to move, he held onto her hips. "Baby, give me a second, or I'll lose it."

She chuckled.

"Go ahead, make fun of me," he teased. "Just wait until you're at the receiving end."

"I *am* at the receiving end," she pointed out.

The distraction her little joke provided helped him gain his composure. "Let's see to it then." Gabriel pulled back, dislodging his cocks but for their heads, before he plunged back in. As he found his rhythm and rode her hard, he marveled at the perfect fit of their bodies. She was truly made for him, her pussy accommodating him in the most perfect way, and her tight ass squeezing him in a way that kept him right at the edge.

The sounds of pleasure coming over her lips warmed his heart and filled him with pride. He was doing this. *He* was giving her pleasure. It was all he could think of. Never had he ridden any woman this hard, this fast, this ferociously. But he was no longer afraid of hurting her. Maya was both a satyr and a vampire, with a body nearly as strong as his, a body built to accommodate him and please him to no end.

For the first time, he silently thanked the

circumstances that had brought them together. Even though what had happened to her was horrible, Gabriel knew it was fate. And he would do anything in his power to make her happy so she would never have to regret her new life. He would give her everything she could ever want.

"I love you," he whispered and plunged deeper. "My wife, my mate, my love."

In his eyes she was already his. The bonding ritual would be only a formality—though a very pleasant and arousing formality.

"Gabriel," she called out before her body suddenly spasmed, her muscles tightening around him. He sensed her orgasm as if he was already bonded to her, felt the waves travel through every cell of her body until they hit him and took him with her. His cocks jerked in unison, pumping hot spurts of seed into her as he came like an exploding volcano, his climax taking over his entire body, sending shockwaves through him that no atomic bomb could produce. His vision blurred, and his mind went blank as he felt his body turn weightless like floating in space.

When he collapsed onto her, he barely had enough strength left in him to roll himself to the side and take her with him so she wouldn't suffer under his weight. For several moments he couldn't speak, could only catch his breath.

He slipped his hand onto her breast and felt her heart beat as frantically as his. Maya's hand came up, and her fingers intertwined with his. She turned her head, and he looked into the eyes of a truly sated woman. It was a look he wanted her to wear every day of their lives together.

A soft brush of his lips against hers was all he could manage. He had no words to describe what he felt, but when he locked eyes with her, he knew she understood. They were one.

~ ~ ~

ABOUT THE AUTHOR

TINA FOLSOM was born in Germany and has been living in English speaking countries for almost her entire adult life.

Tina has always been a bit of a globe trotter: she lived in Germany, Switzerland, England, worked on a cruise ship in the Mediterranean, studied drama and acting at the American Academy of Dramatic Arts in New York and screenwriting in Los Angeles, before meeting the man of her life and following him to San Francisco.

She now lives in an old Victorian in San Francisco with her husband and spends her days writing and translating her own books.

She's always loved vampires, Gods, and other alpha heroes. She has written over 25 books, many of which are available in German, French, and Spanish.

For more about Tina Folsom:

www.tinawritesromance.com

tina@tinawritesromance.com

Twitter: @Tina_Folsom

www.facebook.com/TinaFolsomFans

www.facebook.com/PhoenixCodeSeries

23175148R00114

Printed in Great Britain
by Amazon